ANIMAL QUIZ

ANIMAL QUIZ

Maneka Gandhi

RUPA

Published by
Rupa Publications India Pvt. Ltd.
7/16, Ansari Road, Daryaganj,
New Delhi 110 002

Sales Centres:
Allahabad Bengaluru Chennai
Hyderabad Jaipur Kathmandu
Kolkata Mumbai

To
K.D. SINGH
in gratitude

CONTENTS

INTRODUCTION

When the publishers asked me to write this book, I thought it would be easy. 1000 questions? One week of hard work at the most. It turned out to be a gruelling twelve hours a day for months, poring over animal encyclopedias, animal psychology books, dictionaries, and whatever else I could lay my hands on. My son helped by asking me all the questions he and his friends wanted answered.

It has been a voyage of discovery for me as well. I am slightly wiser, infinitely more interested in an alternate world, a world usually hidden from humans because of the latters' preoccupation with their own species. I hope this book will help you to open your eyes to all the wonderful co-sharers of this world whose lives are as fascinating as ours. By the end of this century you may not see many of these animals and birds any more – unless you show your concern for their protection. Refuse to take part in their exploitation by examining all the things you use – from paintbrushes to doormats to sponges, shoes, cosmetics and anything else that causes the death of a defenceless creature unnecessarily. Have you ever seen a dugong kiss its mate? A bee dance with happiness? A stag show off its antlers proudly? Or a Slender Loris monkey cry? Think how much poorer our world would be without them. Learn about them so that you can help them live.

New Delhi   Maneka Gandhi
January 1989

Some of the questions have more than one answer

1
CLEVER CLEVER

1) Which is the odd one out?
a) Cheetah
b) Serval
c) Lion
d) Jaguar

2) Which is the odd one out?
a) Sea Urchin
b) Dogfish
c) Roach
d) Cockle

3) Which is the odd one out?
a) Dog
b) Elephant
c) Cockroach
d) Emu
e) Trout

4) Which is the odd one out?
a) Lynx
b) Wolf
c) Llama
d) Bear
e) Seal

5) Which is the odd one out?
a) Beetle
b) Spider
c) Dragonfly
d) Mayfly
e) Weevil

6) Which is the odd one out?
a) Emu
b) Kiwi
c) Pigeon
d) Rhea

7) Which is the odd one out?
a) Dugong
b) Olingo
c) Capercaillie
d) Hyrax
e) Pangolin

ANSWERS

1. Serval. The others are known as Big Cats.
2. Roach. It is the only freshwater fish.
3. Cockroach. All the others are vertebrates.
4. Llama. It is the only vegetarian.
5. Spider. All the others are insects.
6. Pigeon. It is the only one that can fly.
7. Capercaillie. It is the only bird.

2
CHAMPS

i) Which is the largest animal in the world?
a) Sibbald's Rorqual *(Balaenoptera musculus)*
b) The African Elephant *(Loxodonta africana)*
c) The Narwhal *(Delphinapterus leucas)*

2) Which is the largest bird alive?
a) The Giant Canada Goose *(Branta canadensis maxima)*
b) The Ostrich *(Struthio camelus)*
c) The Giant Moa *(Dinornis maximus)*

3) Which is the smallest bird of all?
a) The Lesser Pied Kingfisher *(Ceryle rudis)*
b) The Narina Trogon *(Apaloderma narina)*
c) The Bee Hummingbird *(Mellisuga helenae)*
d) The House Martin *(Delichon urbica)*
e) The Little Ringed Plover *(Charidrius dubius)*

4) Which female mammal has the largest litters?
a) The Bush Pig *(Potamochoerus porcus)*
b) The Common Tenrec *(Centetes ecaudatus)*
c) The Babirusa *(Babyrousa babyrussa)*

5) Which animal's milk has the highest amount of sugar in grams per litre?
a) The Goat
b) The Elephant
c) The Whale

6) Which animal's milk has the highest amount of protein in grams per litre?
a) The Porpoise
b) The Pig
c) The Dog

7) Which animal's milk has the highest amount of fat in grams per litre?
a) The Cat
b) The Porpoise
c) The Rhinoceros

8) Which animal's milk is the best balanced per litre?
a) The Camel
b) The Cow
c) The Vole

9) Which is the fiercest animal in the world when cornered?
a) The Common Shrew (*Sorex araneus*)
b) The Honey Badger (*Mellivora capensis*)
c) The Grizzly Bear (*Ursus horribilis*)

10) Which is the most dangerous member of the animal kingdom?
a) The Common Housefly (*Musca domestica*)
b) The Himalayan Viper (*Agkistrodon himalayanus*)
c) The Great Hammerhead Shark (*Sphyrna mokkaran*)

11) Which is the largest order of insects?
a) Flies (Diptera)
b) Beetles (Coleoptera)
c) Earwigs (Dermaptera)

12) Which is the high jump record holder of the animal world?
a) The Flea (Siphonaptera)
b) The True Antelope (Amtilopinae)
c) The Frog (Salientia)

13) Which is the world's largest amphibian?
a) The Chinese Giant Salamander (*Megalobactrus davidianus*)
b) The Andes Toad (*Bufo arunco*)
c) The South American Giant Toad (*Bufo ictericus*)
d) The Mexican Axolot (*Ambystoma mexicanum*)

14) Which is the fastest running bird?
a) The Kori Bustard (*Ardeotis kori*)
b) The Ostrich (*Struthio camelus*)
c) The Ruddy Ground Dove (*Columbigallina talpacoti*)

15) Which bird lays the biggest eggs of all?
a) The Australian Crane (*Grus rubandica*)
b) The Ostrich (*Struthio camelus*)
c) The Great Argus (*Argusianus argus*)

16) Which is the fastest flying bird in the world?
a) The Alpine Spine-Tailed Swift (*Apus melba*)
b) The Kittiwake (*Rissa tridactyla*)
c) The Malabar Trogon (*Harpactus fasciatus*)
d) The Indian Courser (*Cursorius coromandelicus*)

17) Which animal has the largest eyes in the animal kingdom?
a) The African Elephant (*Loxodonta africana*)
b) The Giant Squid (*Architeuthis princeps*)
c) The Blue Whale (*Balaenoptera musculus*)

18) Which is the world's smallest known monkey?
a) The Emperor Tamarin (*Saguinus imperator*)
b) The Japanese Macaque (*Macaca fuscata*)
c) The Pygmy Marmoset (*Cebuella pygmaea*)

19) Which is the heaviest flying bird?
a) The Mute Swan (*Cygnus olor*)
b) The Rhinoceros Auklet (*Cerorhinca monocerata*)
c) The Barn Owl (*Tyto alba*)
d) The Kori Bustard (*Ardeotis kori*)
e) The Great White Pelican (*Pelicanus onocratolus*)
f) The Common Peafowl (*Pavo cristatus*)

20) Which is the largest animal without a backbone?
a) The Giant Scallop (*Pecten maximus*)
b) The Reticulated Python (*Python reticulatus*)
c) The Giant Squid (*Architeuthis princeps*)

21) Which is the heaviest insect in the world?
a) The African Goliath Beetle (*Goliathus meleagris*)
b) The Great Viceroy (*Limenitis populi*)
c) The Greater Wax Moth (*Galleria mellonella*)

22) Which is the longest-living animal recorded?
a) The African Elephant (*Loxodonta africana*)
b) The Galapagos Tortoise (*Testudo elephantopus*)
c) The Sperm Whale (*Physeter catodon*)

23) Which division of the animal world has the sharpest vision?
a) Birds
b) Mammals
c) Fish

24) Which is the largest breed of domesticated cat?
a) Manx
b) Ragdoll
c) Siamese

25) Which bird makes the largest nest?
a) The Social Weaver (*Philetairus socius*)
b) The Black-winged Stilt (*Himantopus himantopus*)
c) The Bald Eagle (*Haliaeetus leucocephalus*)

26) Which is the largest reptile in the world?
a) The Estuarine Crocodile (*Crocodylus porosus*)
b) The Boa Constrictor (*Boa constrictor*)
c) The Gila Monster (*Heloderma suspectum*)

27) Which is the longest venomous snake in the world?
a) The King Cobra (*Ophiophagus hannah*)
b) The Asp Viper (*Vipera aspis*)
c) The Harlequin Coral Snake (*Micrurus fulvius*)

28) Which is the longest of all snakes in the world?
a) The Rubber Boa (*Charina bottae*)
b) The Yellow Anaconda (*Eunectes notaeus*)
c) The Reticulated Python (*Python reticulatus*)

29) Which is the shortest snake in the world?
a) The Thread Snake (*Leptotyphlops bilineata*)
b) The Corn Snake (*Elaphe guttata*)
c) The Linne's Dwarf Snake (*Calamaria linnaei*)

30) Which is the smallest breed of domesticated cat?
a) Abyssinian
b) Singapura
c) Angora

31) Which is the heaviest crustacean in the world?
a) The European Lobster (*Homarus vulgaris*)
b) The Dublin Bay Prawn (*Nephrops norvegicus*)
c) The North Atlantic Lobster (*Homarus americanus*)

32) Which is the tallest living animal?
a) The African Bush Elephant (*Loxodonta africana*)
b) The Giraffe (*Giraffa camelopardalis*)
c) The Giant Squid (*Architeuthis*)

33) Which creature has the most acute sense of smell exhibited in nature?
a) The Eastern Woodrat (*Neotoma floridana*)
b) The Golden Mantled Ground Squirrel (*Citellus lateralis*)
c) The Male Emperor Moth (*Eudia pavonia*)
d) The Silkworm Moth (*Bombyii mori*)
e) The Carrot Fly (*Psila rosae*)

34) Which is the largest land animal?
a) The African Bush Elephant (*Loxodonta africana*)
b) The American Bison (*Bison bison*)
c) The Black Hooklipped Rhinoceros (*Diceros eicornis*)

35) Which is the fastest land animal over a short distance?
a) The Cheetah (*Acinonyx jubatus*)
b) The Gerenuk (*Litocranius walleri*)
c) The Tarpan (*Equus przewalskii przewalskii*)

36) Which mammal has the longest gestation period?
a) The Polar Bear (*Thalarctos maritimus*)
b) The Red Colobus Monkey (*Colobus badius*)
c) The Asian Elephant (*Elephas maximus*)

37) Which animal has the longest horns of any living animal?
a) The Moose (*Alces alces*)
b) The Greater Kudu (*Tragelaphus strepsiceros*)
c) The Water Buffalo (*Bubalus arnee*)

38) Which is the heaviest breed of domestic dog?
a)   The Siberian Husky
b)   The English Mastiff
c)   The St.Bernard
d)   The Alaskan Malamute
e)   The Bull Mastiff

39) Which is the fastest breed of dog?
a)   The Italian Greyhound
b)   The Fox Terrier
c)   The Saluki

40) Which is the tallest breed of domesticated dog?
a)   The Elkhound
b)   The Irish Wolfhound
c)   The Great Dane

41) Which is the smallest breed of domesticated dog?
a)   The Chihuahua
b)   The Yorkshire Terrier
c)   The Toy Poodle

42) Which is considered the smelliest animal in the world?
a)   The Striped Skunk (*Mephites mephites*)
b)   The Warthog (*Phacochoerus aethiopicus*)
c)   The Zorilla (*Ictonyx striatus*)

43) Which bird, known as the feathered locust, is considered the most destructive in the world?
a)   The Redbilled Quelea (*Quelea quelea*)
b)   The Hooded Pitta (*Pitta sordida*)
c)   The Wigeon (*Anas penelope*)

44) Which living bird has the largest wingspan measure-
ment?
a)   The Wandering Albatross (*Diomedia exulans*)
b)   The Andean Condor (*Vultur gryphus*)
c)   The Hooded Vulture (*Neophron monachus*)

45) Which bird lays the largest eggs in relation to its own
size?
a)   The Barnacle Goose (*Branta leucopsis*)
b)   The Common Kiwi (*Apteryx australis*)
c)   The Whistling Swan (*Cygnus columbianus*)

46) Which is the largest domesticated bird?
a)   The Domestic Turkey (*Meleagris gallopavo*)
b)   The Plumed Guineafowl (*Guttera plumifera*)
c)   The Helmeted Guineafowl (*Numida meleagris*)

47) Which is the world's smallest butterfly?
a)   The Dwarf Blue (*Brephidium barberae*)
b)   The Pygmy Blue (*Lycaena exilus*)
c)   The Pale Clouded Yellow (*Colias hylae*)

48) Which bird has the longest feathers?
a)   The Long-tailed Fowl (*Gallus onagadori*)
b)   The Common Peafowl (*Pavo cristatus*)
c)   The Long-tailed Honey Buzzard (*Henicopernis longi-
cauda*)

49) Which snake has the longest fangs?
a)   The Eastern Coral Snake (*Micrurus fulvius*)
b)   The King Cobra (*Ophiophagus hannah*)
c)   The Gaboon Viper (*Bitus gabonica*)

50) Which is the largest bird of prey in the world?
a)   The Andean Condor (*Vultur gryphus*)

b) The King Vulture (*Sarcohamphus papa*)
c) The Golden Eagle (*Aquila chrysaetos*)

51) Which is the fastest-moving land snake in the world?
a) The Black Mamba (*Dendroaspis polylepsis*)
b) The Viperine Grass Snake (*Natrix maura*)
c) The Mangrove Snake (*Boiga dendrophila*)

52) Which is the most poisonous animal ever recorded?
a) The Japanese Pufferfish (*Arothron tetraodon*)
b) The Russell's Viper (*Vipera russelli*)
c) The Kokoi Arrow Poison Frog (*Phyllobates bicolor*)

53) Which has the thickest skin of any living animal?
a) The Giant Girdle-tailed Lizard (*Cordylus giganteus*)
b) The Great African Hippopotamus (*Hippopotamus amphibious*)
c) The Whale Shark (*Rhincondon typus*)

54) Which is the largest known fish in the world?
a) The Whale Shark (*Rhincondon typus*)
b) The Ribbon Tail Ray (*Taeniura lymma*)
c) The Blue Marlin (*Makaira nigricans*)

55) Which living bird lays the smallest egg in proportion to its own size?
a) The Common Partridge (*Perdix perdix*)
b) The Spotted Redshank (*Tringa erythropus*)
c) The Ostrich (*Struthio camelus*)

56) Which is the slowest moving marine fish?
a) The Indo-Pacific Sea Horse (*Hippocampus kuda*)
b) The Spotted Guitarfish (*Rhinobatus lentiginosus*)
c) The Elephant Fish (*Gymnarchus niloticus*)

57) Which is the fastest fish?
a) The Swordfish (*Xiphius gladius*)
b) The Scabbardfish (*Lepidopus caudatus*)
c) The Bonito (*Sarda australis*)
d) The Sailfish (*Istiophorus platypterus*)

58) Which is the most venomous family of fish in the world?
a) Deepsea Viperfishes (Sternoptychidae)
b) Stonefishes (Synanceidae)
c) Surgeonfishes (Acanthuridae)

59) Which is the largest known fly in the world?
a) The Robber Fly (*Mydas heros*)
b) The Horse Fly (*Tabanus sudeticus*)
c) The Drone Fly (*Eristalis tenax*)

60) Which is the largest lizard in the world?
a) The Gila Monster (*Heloderma suspectum*)
b) The Australian Bearded Dragon (*Amphibolurus barbatus*)
c) The Komodo Dragon (*Varanus komodoensis*)

61) Which is the most venomous spider in the world?
a) The Black Widow Spider (*Lactrodectus mactaus*)
b) The Brown Recluse Spider (*Loxosceles reclusa*)
c) The Funnel Web Spider (*Atrax robustus*)

62) Which is the longest lived insect?
a) The Queen Termite (Isoptera)
b) The Male Barklouse (Psocoptera)
c) The Female Lacewing (Neuroptera)

63) Which is the most destructive insect in the world?
a) The Desert Locust (*Schistocerca gregaria*)

b) The Colorado Potato Beetle (*Leptinotarsa decemlineata*)
c) The European Corn Borer Moth (*Ostrinia nubilalis*)

64) Which is the fastest family of fish over a sustained distance?
a) Marlins (Tetrapturus)
b) Snake mackerels (Gemplidae)
c) Cutlass fishes (Trichiurdae)
d) Tunas (Scombridae)

65) Which is the fastest of all land animals over a sustained distance?
a) The Indian Sambar (*Cervus unicolor*)
b) The East Sudan Giant Eland (*Taurotragus oryx*)
c) The Pronghorn Antelope (*Antilocapra americana*)

66) Which animal has the shortest of all mammalian gestation periods?
a) The Common Vole (*Microtus arvalis*)
b) The American Opposum (*Didelphis marsupialis*)
c) The Agouti (*Dasyprocta aguti*)

67) Which mammal has the heaviest brain in relation to its body weight?
a) The Egyptian Jerboa (*Jaculus jaculus*)
b) The Hook-lipped Rhinoceros (*Diceros bicornis*)
c) The Common Marmoset (*Callithrix jacchus*)

68) Which is the largest member of the cat family?
a) The Long Furred Siberian Tiger (*Leo tigris attaica*)
b) The Asiatic Lion (*Panthera leo*)
c) The Puma (*Felis concolor*)

69) Which is the smallest member of the cat family?
a) The Rusty Spotted Cat (*Felis rubiginosa*)
b) The Serval (*Felis serval*)
c) The European Lynx (*Lynx lynx*)

70) Which animals have the most supple spine in the mammalian kingdom?
a) Monk seals (Monachinae)
b) Elephant seals (Cystophorinae)
c) Eared seals (Otariinae)

71) Which is the largest living member of the Monkey family?
a) The Mandrill (*Mandrillus sphinx*)
b) The Red Howler (*Aloutta seniculus*)
c) The Agile Mangabey (*Cercocebus galeritus*)

72) Which mammal has the highest blood temperature?
a) The Banded Mongoose (*Mungos mungo*)
b) The Otter Civet (*Cynogale bennetti*)
c) The Domestic Goat (*Capra hircus*)

73) Which mammal has the lowest blood temperature?
a) The Spiny Anteater (*Tachyglossus aculeatus*)
b) The Brazilian Tapir (*Tapirus terrestris*)
c) The Grysbok (*Raphicerus melanotis*)

74) Which is the oldest known breed of domestic dog?
a) The Cavaliar King Charles Spaniel
b) The Arabian Gazelle Hound
c) The Italian Greyhound

75) Which are the rarest recognized breeds of domestic dog?
a) Chinese Crested Dog

b) Lowchen or Lion Dog
c) Hungarian Vizsla

76) Which mammals have the shortest lifespan?
a) Shrews
b) Ferrets
c) Chamois

77) Which is the world's smallest mammal?
a) The Pygmy Marmoset (*Cebuella pygmaea*)
b) Savi's Pygmy Shrew (*Sorex minutus*)
c) The Water Vole (*Arvicola amphibius*)

78) Which mammal weighs the least in the world?
a) The European Common Mole (*Talpa europaea*)
b) The Least Weasel (*Mustela rixosa*)
c) The Lesser Gymnure (*Hylomys suillus*)

79) Which animals have the highest number of litters in a year?
a) Rabbits
b) Mice
c) Guinea Pigs

80) Which is the longest-living bird?
a) The Imperial Eagle (*Aquila imperialis*)
b) The Blue Macaw (*Ara macao*)
c) The European Eagle-Owl (*Bubo bubo*)

81) Which is the most poisonous fish in the world?
a) Japanese Pufferfish (*Arothron tetraodon*)
b) The Convict Tang (*Acanthurus stegus*)
c) The Devilfish (*Mobula mobulari*)

82) Which is the fastest moving land snake in the world?
a) The African Fork-Marked Grass Snake (*Psammophis furcatus*)
b) The Black Mamba (*Dendoaspis polylepis*)
    British Grass Snake (*Natrix natrix*)

83) Which is the largest land crab in the world?
a) The King Crab (*Paralithodes camtschatica*)
b) The Coconut Crab (*Birgus latro*)
c) The Red Land Crab (*Gigantinus lateralis*)

84) Which is the largest crustacean in the world?
a) The Giant Spider Crab (*Macrocheira kaempferi*)
b) The Large Slipper Lobster (*Seyllarides latus*)
c) The European Stone Crab (*Lithodes maia*)

ANSWERS

1. a	2. b	3. c	4. b	5. b	6. a
7. b	8. b	9. a	10. a	11. b	12. a
13. a	14. b	15. b	16. a	17. b	18. c
19. d	20. c	21. a	22. b	23. a	24. b
25. c	26. a	27. a	28. c	29. a	30. b
31. c	32. b	33. c	34. a	35. a	36. c
37. c	38. c	39. c	40. b	41. a	42. c
43. a	44. a	45. b	46. a	47. a	48. a
49. c	50. a	51. a	52. c	53. c	54. a
55. c	56. a	57. d	58. b	59. a	60. c
61. a	62. a	63. a	64. a	65. c	66. b
67. c	68. a	69. a	70. b	71. a	72. c
73. a	74. b	75. ab	76. a	77. b	78. a
79. a	80. c	81. a	82. b	83. b	84. a

3
USE AND ABUSE

1) How do collectors catch the Giant Birdwing Butterfly
   which measures 12" across its wingspan and flies on
   the tops of trees?
a) They climb trees and net it
b) They shoot it with water guns
c) They trap it with nets stretched across the trees

2) Which city holds an annual Insect Trading Day when
   insects are bought and sold?
a) Frankfurt
b) Dhaka
c) Hongkong

3) People use sponges as mops and swabs. What is a
   sponge?
a) The skeleton of the sea cucumber (*Pentacta tuberculosa*)
b) A multicelled invertebrate animal (*Phylum porifera*)
c) The Luminescent Jellyfish (*Pelagia noctiluca*)

4) Which marine animals are dried, ground and made
   into poultry meal and fertilizer?
a) Combfishes (Zaniolepididae)
b) Swamp Eels (Synbranchidae)
c) Horse Mussels (Modiolae)

5) Which form of marine life was used in early India as
   coins?
a) Clams
b) Cockle shells
c) Cowrie shells

6) How are baby seals killed to make sealcoats?
a) They are shot in the head and then skinned
b) They are fed poisoned fish and then skinned
c) They are clubbed repeatedly and then skinned alive

7) How many dik-diks (dwarf antelopes) are killed to make a pair of gloves?
a) One
b) Eight
c) Two

8) Which rodent's skin is used by humans for fur?
a) The Coypu (*Myocastor coypus*)
b) The Lesser Cane Rat (*Thryonomys gregorianus*)
c) The Guinea Pig (*Cavia aperea porcellus*)

9) The oil of which fish is used in the oiling of precision equipment?
a) Oil Sardines (Clupeiformes)
b) Ratfish (Chimaeriformes)
c) Oilfishes (Scorpaeniformes)

10) The excrement of seabirds is used as commercial fertilizer. What is it called?
a) Guano
b) Phosphos
c) Nauru

11) What is deer meat called?
a) Bacon
b) Venison
c) Haggis

12) What animal does the toy Teddy Bear represent?
a) A baby Bear
b) A Koala
c) A Panda

13) The rhinoceros is killed by poachers for a small part of its body supposed, erroneously, to be an aphrodisiac. Which part is it?
a) Tail
b) Horn
c) The musk sac under its front hooves

14) Which harmless animal is killed so that its fur can be used to make doormats?
a) The Common Wombat (*Vombatus hirsutus*)
b) The Moonrat (*Echinosorex gymnurus*)
c) The European Hedgehog (*Erinaceus europeus*)

15) Expensive quilts have a soft stuffing in them called eiderdown. From which creature is it obtained?
a) The Eiderlamb
b) The Eiderduck
c) The Eidergoat

16) In the U.S.S.R. which animal fur is used for lining military clothing?
a) The Rat Chinchilla (*Abrocoma cinerea*)
b) The Raccoon Dog (*Nyctereutes procyonoides*)
c) The Arctic Lemming (*Dicrostonyx torquatus*)

17) Which animal's skin was prized as the most valuable parchment in the Middle East?
a) The Dog
b) The Donkey
c) The Pig

18) Which birds' nests are made of gluey saliva and form the main ingredient of the Chinese Bird's Nest Soup?
a) Coucals
b) Swiftlets
c) Goatsuckers

19) Which sheep gives the finest wool?
a) The Merino
b) The Corridale
c) The Angora

20) What is Caviar made of?
a) The eggs of the Royal Sturgeon (*Huso huso*)
b) The eggs of European Green Lizards (*Lacerta viridis*)
c) The Common or Edible Sea Urchin (*Echinus esculentus*)

21) The 'Bozoar stone' was once regarded, mistakenly, as an antidote to poison. Which animal was it extracted from?
a) The King Cobra (*Ophiophagus hannah*)
b) The Wild Goat (*Capra aegagrus*)
c) The Chamois Goat (*Rupicapra rupicapra*)

22) Which animals in India are captured and beaten at regular intervals while their scent pouches are scraped for their extract for perfume?
a) The Large Indian Civet (*Viverra zibetha*)
b) The Musk Deer (*Moschus moschiferus*)
c) The Musk Ox (*Ovibos moschatus*)

22) How many minks have to be killed for a fur coat?
a) 1-5
b) 10-15
c) 60-80

23) Which animal's hide was copied as camouflage for jungle warfare uniforms in World War II?
a) The Zebra
b) The Leopard
c) The Spotted Hyena

24) How many caterpillars of the Silkmoth *Bombyx mori* have to be boiled alive for one pound of silk?
a) 3000
b) 100
c) 1000

25) Which insect is dried and pulverized to produce the carmine red dye cochineal?
a) The Mealybug (*Dactylopius indicus*)
b) The Cotton Stainer Bug (*Dysdercus suturellus*)
c) The Brassica Bug (*Eurydema oleraceum*)

26) One of the enzymes used for the fermentation of beer comes from the lungs of a creature. Which creature is it?
a) Fish
b) Insect
c) Reptile

27) Manna is supposed to have been the miraculous food given to the children of Israel. What was it?
a) The wings of the Moroccan migratory locust (*Stauronotus marroccanus*)
b) The royal jelly of the cells of the Mason Bee (Osmia) hives
c) A secretion exuded by tamarisk trees when pierced by scaly insects (Homoptera)

28) How is lacquer or shellac produced?
a)   From the skin of the Lachninae family of aphids
b)   From the eggs of the Laccobius species of beetles
c)   From the skeleton of the scale insect Laccifer lacca

29) How many insects are killed to make one kilo of shellac?
a)   20
b)   7500
c)   200,000

30) Recently, an American manufacturer ordered 140,000 skins of this harmless Australian animal to make into ski apparel. Which animal was it?
a)   The Grey Kangaroo (*Macropus giganteus ocydromus*)
b)   The Marsupial Anteater (*Myrmecobius fasciatus*)
c)   The Golden Frog (*Hyla aurea*)

31) Which substance obtained from killing a species of deer is used in perfume?
a)   Deerwax
b)   Musk
c)   Odourismus

32) From which creature is ambergris, used as a fixative in perfumes, obtained?
a)   The Skunk Dolphin (*Cephalorhynchus commersonii*)
b)   The Sperm Whale (*Physeter catodon*)
c)   The Necklace Sloth (*Bradypus torquatus*)

33) Quicklime and cement use which animal species as raw material?
a)   Beetle cuticles
b)   Mollusc shells
c)   Turtle carapaces

34) Which creature was used in the practice of phlebotomy (bloodletting) described as a cure for all diseases ranging from delirium to gout?
a) The Medicine Leech (*Hirundinaria granulosa*)
b) The Indian Vampire Bat (*Megaderma lyra*)
c) The Robber Fly (*Asilidae*)

35) Which of these jewellery items come from the death of an animal?
a) Coral
b) Pearl
c) Opal
d) Cat's Eye

36) Which member of the animal world gives us Royal Jelly used in medicine?
a) The Jellyfish
b) The Honeybee
c) The Royal Spoonbill bird

37) Which Asian animal's three-day-old young are slaughtered for astrakhan fur to make hats?
a) The Karakul Sheep
b) The Jaguarundi (*Herpailurus yagouaroundi*)
c) The Snow Hare (*Lepus timidus*)

38) Which Asian animal is caught and beaten repeatedly till it dies because its tears are regarded as love potions?
a) The Dayan Hare (*Lepus dayanus*)
b) The Dugong (*Dugong dugong*)
c) The Side-striped Jackal (*Canis adustus*)

39) Which animal's extract is used by the Javanese to flavour tobacco?
a) The Coypu

b) The Civet
c) The Javan Ferret Badger

40) From which animal does pashmina wool come from?
a) The Barbary Sheep (*Amorotragus lervia*)
b) The Siberian Ibex (*Capra ibex sibirica*)
c) The Markhor (*Capra falconeri*)

41) Which animal, enormously useful as a natural land-scaper and protector of the mountains, is killed in the thousands because its tail tastes like a fish and its scent glands are erroneously considered 'wonder medicine'?
a) The Beaver (Castoridae)
b) The Mountain Beaver (Aplodontoidae)
c) The Hutia (Capromyidae)

42) A major part of the economy of the Mongolian People's Republic depends on the export of two million animal skins annually of just one wild animal. Which is it?
a) The Bobac Marmot (*Marmota bobac sibirica*)
b) The Shensi Takin (*Budorcas taxicolor bedfordi*)
c) The Spotted Souslik (*Citellus suslicus*)

ANSWERS

1. b	2. a	3. b	4. c	5. c	6. c
7. c	8. a	9. b	10. a	11. b	12. b
13. b	14. a	15. b	16. b	17. b	18. b
19. a	20. a	21. b	22. c	23. b	24. a
25. a	26. a	27. c	28. c	29. c	30. a
31. b	32. b	33. b	34. a	35. ab	36. b
37. a	38. b	39. b	40. b	41. a	42. a

4
LANGUAGE

1) The word Vet is short for animal doctor. What is the full word?
a) Veterinarian
b) Veterologist
c) Veteratian

2) What is a fox's tail called?
a) A Tail
b) A Brush
c) A Tangle

3) What is a Sett?
a) The burrow of a badger
b) The young of a squirrel
c) The home of a beaver

4) What does the word Termite mean?
a) End
b) Wood-eater
c) False ant

5) What is a female Ass called?
a) Jenny
b) Jackanne
c) Assinine

6) What is the offspring of a Tiger and a Lion called?
a) Tiglon
b) Ligon
c) Tigel
d) Litiger

7) What does the word Reptile mean?
a) To creep
b) With fangs
c) Scaly

8) What does the word Rodent mean?
a) To gnaw
b) To cause harm
c) To scurry

9) Which animal's home is called a Drey?
a) Jackal
b) Squirrel
c) Marmot

10) What is a group of Lions called?
a) A pride
b) A regiment
c) A roar

11) What is a group of Baboons called?
a) A jabber
b) A troop
c) A contail

12) What does the word Dinosaur mean?
a) Extinct species
b) Large creatures
c) Terrible lizards

13) What is a nest of eggs called?
a) A home
b) A grab
c) A clutch

14) What does the word Orangutan mean?
a) Orange monkey
b) Man of the woods
c) Hairy man

15) What are antler branches called?
a) Twigs
b) Tines
c) Forks

16) What is the product of a Gaur and a domestic Cow called in Assam?
a) Mithan
b) Gaurgai
c) Gurial

17) What is a Zo?
a) An animal born in a zoo
b) The offspring of a male yak and a domestic cow
c) An animal that has been artificially neutered

18) Where does the word Civet come from?
a) It is Arabic for scent from the glands
b) It is Greek for noxious
c) It is Latin for catlike

19) What were Bats commonly called before their species was classified?
a) Vampire owls
b) Flittermice
c) Night kelpies

20) What is a Pig's enclosure called?
a) A piggery

b) A sty
c) A hogpound

21) What is the person who shoes a horse called?
a) A smith
b) A farrier
c) A shoemaker

22) What does the word Amphibia mean?
a) Living in water
b) Having two lives
c) Scaled

23) The word Bandicoot (Peramelidae) comes from a corruption of the Telugu word Pandi-kokku. What does the word mean?
a) Pig-rat
b) Long-toothed
c) Mouse-shrew

24) What is a group of Whales called?
a) A school
b) A gam
c) A whoosh

25) What is a group of Kittens called?
a) A kindle
b) A mess
c) A smelt

26) What is a group of Leopards called?
a) A growth
b) A gash
c) A leap

27) What is a group of Nightingales called?
a) A warble
b) A watch
c) A choir

28) What is a young Partridge called?
a) A tweeter
b) A partlet
c) A cheeper

29) What is a young Rooster called?
a) A cockerel
b) A chicklet
c) A roster

30) What is a young Swan called?
a) A cygnet
b) A swain
c) A swanlet

31) What is a young Fish called?
a) A fishlet
b) A fingerling
c) A fillet

32) What is a young Hare called?
a) A harnet
b) A herendon
c) A leveret

33) What is a young Frog called?
a) A froggle
b) A polliwog
c) A tadpole

34) What is a young Pigeon called?
a)   A swab
b)   A scrub
c)   A baguette

35) What is a young Kangaroo called?
a)   A roo
b)   A joey
c)   A pouchbaby

36) What is a young Eel called?
a)   An elt
b)   An elver
c)   An elmer

37) Which is faster – a Jackal or a Rabbit?
a)   Jackal
b)   Rabbit
c)   Both are the same

38) What does the word 'fossil' mean?
a)   To dig
b)   Preserved
c)   Remains

39) What is the science of Fossils called?
a)   Anthropometry
b)   Orthodontology
c)   Palaeontology

40) What does the word Hamster mean?
a)   Burrower
b)   Hoarder
c)   Digger

41) What does the word Langur mean?
a) Banana-eater
b) Red-bottomed
c) Long-tailed

42) What does the word Cephalopod mean?
a) Many-headed
b) Many-eyed
c) Head-footed

43) What is a collection of Gnats called?
a) A burst
b) A swarm
c) A cloud

44) What is a group of Boars called?
a) A party
b) A sounder
c) A hubbub

45) What is a group of Cats called?
a) A clutter
b) A mangle
c) A macavity

46) What is a group of Asses called?
a) A pace
b) A quarry
c) A scrimshaw

47) What is a group of Crows called?
a) A hatchet
b) A coffret
c) A murder

48) What is a group of Ferrets called?
a) A labyrinth
b) A business
c) A nutation

49) What is a group of Foxes called?
a) A prowl
b) A quire
c) A skulk

50) What is a group of Jellyfish called?
a) A quiver
b) A stuck
c) A squish

51) What is a group of Snakes called?
a) A den
b) A roll
c) A wriggle

52) What is a group of Toads called?
a) A bulletin
b) A bush
c) A knot

53) What is a group of Peacocks called?
a) A blaze
b) A muster
c) A virgule

54) What is a group of Ravens called?
a) A harvest
b) An unkindness
c) A thunder

1. a	2. b	3. a	4. a	5. a	6. b
7. a	8. a	9. b	10. a	11. b	12. c
13. c	14. b	15. b	16. a	17. b	18. a
19. b	20. b	21. b	22. b	23. a	24. b
25. a	26. c	27. b	28. c	29. a	30. a
31. b	32. c	33. b	34. a	35. b	36. c
37. c	38. a	39. c	40. b	41. c	42. c
43. c	44. b	45. a	46. a	47. c	48. b
49. c	50. b	51. a	52. c	53. b	54. b

5
TRAVELLERS' GUIDE

1) From which country do practically all the natural sponges come?
a) Mauritius
b) Greece
c) Japan

2) Which was India's first National Park?
a) Kaziranga National Park in Assam
b) Corbett National Park in Uttar Pradesh
c) Kanha National Park in Madhya Pradesh

3) Where did goldfish come from originally?
a) Malaysia
b) China
c) New Zealand

4) Which country has the largest domestic cat population?
a) Britain
b) France
c) The United States of America

5) Which is the National Bird of India?
a) The Sarus Crane (*Grus antigone*)
b) The Common Peafowl (*Pavo cristatus*)
c) The Great Indian Bustard (*Choriotis nigriceps*)

6) In which European country does the matador still kill bulls for sport by piercing them with knives and swords?
a) Spain
b) Holland
c) Finland

7) The llama, a relation of the camel, is found in only one continent. Which one?
a) Australia
b) South America
c) Africa

8) Papua and New Guinea are famous for being the habitat of the most beautiful birds in the world. What are they?
a) Birds of Paradise (Paradisaeinae)
b) Babbling Thrushes (Timaliinae)
c) Sunbirds (Nectariniidae)

9) From where in the world did all the zoo bred white tigers come from?
a) Jersey, England
b) Rewa, India
c) Siberia, U.S.S.R.

10) Which bird is the heraldic symbol of Japan?
a) The Japanese Quail (*Coturnix coturnix japonica*)
b) The Japanese Ibis (*Nipponia nippon*)
c) The Japanese Cormorant (*Phalacrocorax capillatus*)
d) The Japanese Bittern (*Gorsachius goisagi*)

11) Which islands are called a world in itself for the large number of fauna unique to them?
a) Galapagos Islands
b) South Pacific Islands
c) Maldive Islands

12) Tenrecs (small animals resembling hedgehogs) are only found in one island of the world. Which one?
a) Corfu
b) Madagascar
c) Isle of Man

13) Which type of squirrel inhabits your garden in India?
a) The Hoar-bellied Squirrel
b) The Malayan Giant Squirrel
c) The Five-Striped Palm Squirrel

14) What is a urial and where is it found?
a) A black bear of Sikkim, Bhutan and Tibet
b) A wild sheep of Punjab, Sind and Baluchistan
c) A scavenging bird of the Andes

15) Which is the second largest animal of India?
a) The Indian Elephant
b) The Indian One-horned Rhinoceros
c) The Gangetic Dolphin

16) Which animal is often kept as a pet in Indian villages to control rats, mice and scorpions?
a) The Striped Hyena (*Hyaena hyaena*)
b) The Indian Brown Mongoose (*Herpestes fuscus*)
c) The Indian Wolf (*Canis lupus pallipes*)

17) Where are Yak found?
a) Ladakh, India
b) Tibet
c) Kansu Province, China
d) Siberia
c) The Peruvian Andes

18) Where is the main rhinoceros sanctuary of India?
a) Kaziranga, Assam
b) Pocharam, Andhra Pradesh
c) Baishipali, Orissa

19) Which countries are supposed to have been the original homes of the Common House Rat (*Rattus rattus*)
a) Burma
b) Britain
c) Norway
d) India
e) Afghanistan

20) Which animal forms 98% of the rodent population in Calcutta?
a) The Eastern House Mouse (*Mus musculus domesticus*)
b) The House Rat (*Rattus rattus*)
c) The Brown Rat (*Rattus norvegicus*)

21) In which country are hyenas eaten?
a) Bhutan

b) Egypt
c) Kenya

22) Which part of the planet Earth is the New World?
a) All the lands that make up the American Continents
b) All the land around the two poles
c) Canada, North America and Europe

23) Which continent is believed to be the original home of the mongoose?
a) South America
b) Africa
c) Europe

24) Where did the Dodo live?
a) Mauritius
b) Corfu
c) Maldives

25) Roman coins of 74 B.C. depict a man riding an animal. Which animal is it?
a) Dolphin
b) Horse
c) Dragon

26) Which city of the United States was named after a much disliked but perfectly harmless animal?
a) Chicago – the Sikako or Skunk
b) Dallas – the Dallia or Coyote
c) Newark – the Arko or the Great Auk bird

27) A certain animal is only found in two places of the world -- Southern U.S.A. and the Yangtse Valley in China. What is it?
a) The Mandarin Duck (*Aix galericulata*)

b) The Alligator (*Alligator mississipiensis*)
c) The Lesser Flamingo (*Phoenichonaias minor*)

28) Which bird has been a heraldic symbol for these countries and empires -- Czarist Russia, the Austrian Empire, Napoleonic France, the Prussian Empire and the Roman Empire?
a) Great Black Hawk (*Buteogallus urubitinga*)
b) The Osprey (*Pandion haliaetus*)
c) The Golden Eagle (*Aquila chrysaetos*)

29) Which bird figures on the Great Seal of the United States of America?
a) The Bald Eagle (*Haliaeetus leucocephalus*)
b) The American Kestrel (*Falco sparverius*)
c) The American Wigeon (*Anas americanus*)

30) Which city had a school for dancing horses and what was it called?
a) Vienna, Lipizzaner
b) Rome, Equus
c) Moscow, Orlov

31) Which animal is only found in the Little Rann of Kutch?
a) The Slender Loris (*Loris tardigradus*)
b) The Asiatic Wild Ass (*Equus hemonius*)
c) The Desert Lynx (*Caracal caracal*)

32) Which rodent is the greatest pest of South-east Asia?
a) The Pygmy Mouse (*Baiomys taylori*)
b) The Little Rat (*Raatus exulans*)
c) The Lesser Bandicoot Rat (*Bandicota bengalensis*)

33) What is India's National Animal?
a)   The Tiger
b)   The Pangolin
c)   The Hanuman Langur

34) Where in India is Hoolock's Gibbon found?
a)   The Nilgiri hills
b)   The Vindhya range of mountains
c)   The mountain forests of Assam

35) Which animal is the Dumkhar Sanctuary meant to
     protect?
a)   The Chinkara
b)   The Sloth Bear
c)   The Black Buck

36) Which country's government exterminated tigers as
     'harmful to agricultural and pastoral progress'?
a)   Zaire
b)   China
c)   Iraq

37) Where is the world's greatest stony coral structure?
a)   The coral reefs of the Andaman Islands
b)   The coral reefs in the Red Sea
c)   The Great Barrier Reefs in Queensland

38) What is the State Bird of Punjab?
a)   The Indian Pitta (*Pitta brachyura*)
b)   The Dabchick (*Pondiceps ruficollis*)
c)   The Eastern Goshawk (*Accipiter baz*)
d)   The Brahminy Kite (*Haliastur indus*)

39) What is the State Animal of Punjab?
a) The Black Buck Antelope (*Antilope cervicapra*)
b) The Indian Wild Boar (*Sus scrofa cristatus*)
c) The Sand Cat (*Felis margharita*)

40) What is the National Bird of America?
a) The Californian Condor (*Gymnogyps californianus*)
b) The Bald Eagle (*Haliaeetus leucocephalus*)
c) The Imperial Eagle (*Aquila heliaca*)

41) Which bird is the heraldic symbol of Guatemala whose monetary unit is also named for it?
a) The Corncrake (*Crex crex*)
b) The Quetzal (*Pharomachrus mocino*)
c) The Imperial Parrot (*Amazona imperialis*)

42) In which country is the largest scorpion in the world found?
a) Iran
b) India
c) Indonesia

43) Where is the Go-Away bird found?
a) Central Africa
b) South America
c) Eastern Europe

44) Which animal was considered the royal and sacred creature of Thailand?
a) The Eastern Bluebird (*Sialia sialis*)
b) The Siamese Cat
c) The Siamang Gibbon (*Hylobates syndactylus*)

45) To which countries do these breeds of horses belong?

a)	Murgese	a)	Italy
b)	Gelderland	b)	U.S.A.
c)	Morgan	c)	Turkey
d)	Carthusian	d)	Indonesia
e)	Lusitano	e)	U.S.S.R.
f)	Orlov	f)	Portugal
g)	Karacabey	g)	Holland
h)	Sandalwood	h)	Spain

46) Where are the headquarters of the World Wildlife Fund?
a) New York, U.S.A.
b) Vienna, Austria
c) Gland, Switzerland

47) Where is the Katarniaghat Crocodile Sanctuary, known to have the largest collection of Gharials?
a) Visakhapatnam, Andhra Pradesh
b) Aurangabad, Maharashtra
c) Bahraich, Uttar Pradesh

48) Which sanctuary serves as the last refuge of the Hangul?
a) Dachigam National Park, Kashmir
b) Bhagwan Mahavir National Park, Goa
c) Simlipal National Park in Orissa

49) Which is the only sanctuary to have Asiatic Lions?
a) Gir National Park and Reserve in Gujarat
b) Neyyar Reserve in Kerala
c) Kumbhalgarh Reserve in Rajasthan

50) Which National Park in India is famous for its large number of Swamp Deer?
a) Mudumalai Tiger Reserve, Tamil Nadu
b) Kinnersani Reserve, Andhra Pradesh
c) Dudhwa National Park in Uttar Pradesh

51) Which sanctuary in India contains almost all the entire population of the endangered species Nilgiri Tahr?
a) Kalakkadu Reserve, Tamil Nadu
b) Bannarghatta National Park, Karnataka
c) Eravikulam National Park, Kerala

52) Which of the tiger reserves in India has been described as the best place for the viewing of tigers?
a) Ranthambhor Tiger Sanctuary in Rajasthan
b) Kanha National Park in Madhya Pradesh
c) Manas Tiger Reserve in Assam

53) In 1938 the Viceroy and his party shot 4273 birds in one day at a place now protected as a bird sanctuary. Which is it?
a) Nalsarowar Bird Reserve, Gujarat
b) Ranganathittu Bird Reserve, Karnataka
c) Keoladeo Ghana Bird Sanctuary, Bharatpur

ANSWERS

1. b	2. b	3. b	4. c	5. b	6. a
7. b	8. a	9. b	10. b	11. a	12. b
13. c	14. b	15. b	16. b	17. ab	18. a
19. ad	20. c	21. b	22. a	23. b	24. a
25. a	26. a	27. b	28. c	29. a	30. a
31. b	32. c	33. a	34. c	35. b	36. b
37. c	38. c	39. a	40. b	41. b	42. b

43. a   44. b   45. a-a, b-g, c-b, d-h, e-f, f-e, g-c, h-d
46. c   47. c   48. a   49. a   50. c   51. c
52. b   53. c

6
ANIMALS ARE PEOPLE TOO

1) What do most species of deer do when alarmed, to warn
    the group?
a) They start running around the group
b) They raise their tails to show the rump patches
c) They make a barking sound

2) Why do dogs pant?
a) Having almost no sweat glands, they are cooled by the
    evaporation of water from the mouth
b) It is an expression of distress
c) To gulp larger amounts of air after any strenuous
    exercise

3) Why do animals fluff up their hair in cold weather?
a) To trap a greater layer of warm air
b) To cover those areas of their bodies which are exposed
    to the cold
c) So that cold moisture falls on the extended hair and
    does not reach the skin

4) When you reprimand a dog severely it will look away
    and raise a forepaw. What does this action mean?
a) It is ignoring you
b) It shows complete submission
c) It wants you to play

5) What is a horse signalling when its ears twitch back and forth independent of each other?
a) Contentment
b) Anger
c) Hunger

6) What is a horse most likely to do when both its ears are laid back flat?
a) Feed
b) Rebel, attack and bite
c) Nuzzle up and lick

7) Horses neigh in different ways to communicate a feeling. If the neigh is long, high-pitched and repeated at regular intervals, what does it mean?
a) Extreme fear
b) Well-being and contentment
c) It is a mating call

8) The female of the Ground Squirrel family *(Smermophilus beldingi),* which lives in groups, has only one litter a year. If she loses it through predation what does she do?
a) She goes into oestrus again and has another litter
b) She bangs her head repeatedly against a rock till she dies
c) She moves to another area and slaughters all the infant squirrels existing in the new group

9) The Warthog *(Phacochoerus aethiopicus)* is the only species of pig who does this while searching for food. What is the characteristic?
a) It moves on its wrists
b) It uses its teeth for digging instead of its snout
c) It moves backwards with its head lowered

10) Kangaroos lick their arms and chests repeatedly. Why?
a) To keep them clean
b) The evaporated mucus helps cool the body temperature
c) To prevent the loss of salt

11) How does a dog mark the path that he has travelled?
a) By urinating along the route
b) By rubbing his nose at selected points along the route
c) By leaving his droppings along the route

12) Bats are considered creatures of the dark. How do they react to light?
a) They retreat into dark caves during the hours of light
b) They have no objection to light. It is changes in temperature that affect them
c) They cannot bear light and even when flying in the daytime keep their eyes shut tightly, using their echolocation to guide them

13) How does the porcupine attack?
a) It stands still and shoots its quills at the enemy
b) It jumps on the enemy and buries its spines in it
c) It launches itself backwards into the enemy

14) What do the lemurs do with their long tails when they sleep?
a) They wrap them round their necks
b) They hang by them
c) They curl them round their legs

15) The word glutton has come to mean one who eats enormously. What does the Glutton do actually?
a) It challenges much larger carnivores like bears and wolves and carries away their prey

b) It kills far more than it can eat and refuses to let any other carnivore touch its uneaten prey
c) It vomits its undigested food

16) In the absence of water what do elephants spray themselves with?
a) Dust
b) Urine
c) Dew

17) In the rare event of a fight between an elephant and a rhinoceros, the latter is usually killed. What does the elephant do then?
a) It stamps on it till the horn breaks
b) It covers the body totally with branches and twigs
c) It walks away ignoring the body

18) The expression 'bearhug' comes from the belief that bears hug for various reasons. Which of these?
a) The belief is a fallacy
b) They hug each other while mating
c) They hug their victims and squeeze them to death

19) When do lions roar most mightily?
a) Shortly after sunset for one hour
b) After they have eaten their prey
c) Early in the morning

20) What facial behaviour of the cat indicates that it is afraid?
a) Its round pupils become longer and its ears perk up
b) It slits its eyes and dilates its nostrils
c) It yawns widely

21) When these animals are threatened they do not flee. They form a closed circle keeping their young in the centre. Which animals are these?
a) Elephants
b) Hedgehogs
c) Wild Asses

22) How does the lead cow elephant control the fear or uncertainty on the part of a group member?
a) She hits it with her trunk
b) She shoves a bundle of grass into its mouth
c) She raises her trunk and snorts

23) What happens when a female fox mother is shot?
a) The male fox abandons the pups
b) The male fox kills the pups
c) The male fox takes over the nurture of the pups

24) What does a pointer dog do?
a) It captures the shot quarry for its owner
b) It indicates the direction of the quarry without going after it itself
c) It guides the blind

25) How do zebras greet each other?
a) They rear up on their hind legs
b) They snort and sneeze
c) They sniff noses and bellies

26) If a gorilla looks directly at another gorilla what does it mean?
a) It is a mating call
b) Threat
c) Sign of recognition

27) The leader of the wolf pack is the only one allowed to adopt a certain posture. What is it?
a) To have his ears erect
b) To have his tail raised above the level of his back
c) To have his neck raised at an angle

28) To the young of which animal does this refer to: It grasps a mammilla in its mouth. This is ringed by a powerful muscle. The baby does not leave it during the entire period of gestation. It has no power to suck and would die but for the muscular action of the mammae which from time to time squirt milk into its mouth.
a) The young of the anteater
b) The young of the kangaroo
c) The young of the hyrax

29) What did Ivan Petrovitch Pavlov's experiments with dogs show?
a) Disordered behaviour due to a toxic process
b) Conditioned reflexes
c) Communication between different species

30) Why does the cat's/dog's hair stand on end when attacking or faced with an adversary?
a) The muscles of the hair roots contract due to a lowering of the blood temperature causing them to stand on end
b) Tension causes a rise in blood temperature which expands the muscles of the hair roots causing the hair to stand on end
c) Tension causes adrenaline to be released and this acts on the muscles of the hair roots causing them to stand on end

31) Does the vampire bat really suck its victim's blood after it punctures the skin with its incisor teeth?
a) Yes

b) No, it merely laps it up
c) False vampire bats do not suck, true ones do

32) In 24 hours how many hours do cats sleep?
a) 9
b) 16
c) 12

33) Dugongs eat algae, seaweed and seagrasses. How do these sirenians rid their food of sand and poisonous marine mammals before they eat it?
a) They shake the bundles of grass/algae about till all the sand and creatures have fallen out
b) They pile up their torn out food on the floor in stacks and let it be for some time till the sand has settled and the creatures have moved out
c) They bring their food to the shores of the river and pile it till it is dry. Then they shake it and eat it

34) Starfish (Asteroida) are carnivores. While some catch prey with their long arms, others have an extraordinary method. What is it?
a) They push their stomachs out, wrap it round their prey and start to digest it. When it is partly digested the stomach and the bits of food are retracted
b) They attach the suckers of their arms to their prey and digestive juices come out through the sucker pods to dissolve it partially before they ingest it
c) They squirt stomach juices at a passing prey. This has an instant partial dissolving effect. While the prey is stunned, the arms are wrapped round it and it is ingested

35) What do Sea Cucumbers (Holothuroidea) do when threatened?
a) They squirt a green-coloured ink and scurry away
b) They eject and abandon their entire gut and creep away to grow another set
c) They enlarge themselves to six times their size and push out prickly growths

36) The Pistol or Snapping Shrimp has an enormous claw – almost half as big as its body – which it extends in front to catch small fish. How does it do that?
a) When close to its stalked prey it dislocates its claw, stunning it with the loud report produced and when the fish tips over it catches it
b) It waves its claw frantically once it is close to its prey and the fish is dislocated by the movement of water and tips over
c) It stays motionless until the prey comes close and then opens its claw suddenly, grabbing the unsuspecting fish

ANSWERS

1. b	2. a	3. a	4. b	5. b	6. b
7. b	8. c	9. a	10. b	11. a	12. b
13. c	14. a	15. a	16. a	17. b	18. a
19. a	20. a	21. a	22. b	23. c	24. b
25. c	26. b	27. b	28. b	29. b	30. c
31. b	32. b	33. b	34. a	35. b	36. a

7
SCIENTIFIC NAMES

1) If diurnal means daytime animals and nocturnal night, what is crepuscular?
a) Twilight
b) Dawn
c) Moonlit

2) In what units is the height of a horse usually measured?
a) Feet
b) Hands
c) Inches

3) What is Ecdysis?
a) The shedding of an outer coat by snakes, crustaceans and insects
b) The increase and change of colour of mating plumage in birds
c) The settlement of an immigrant bird in a new environment

4) When a Zebra foal is born it recognizes every large object as its mother. Only after a few days does it learn irrevocably which its mother is. What is this recognition called?
a) Imprinting
b) Foaling
c) Naturalization

5) What does Ethology mean?
a) The study of the successful relocation of entire species to another habitat

b) The study of moral behaviour in wild animals
c) The study of animal behaviour in relation to habitat

6) Invertebrata and Chordata. What is special about these terms?
a) They are the two main divisions of the animal kingdom
b) They are the two main divisions of sea animals
c) They are the two main divisions of the mammal kingdom

7) What does an angler call the bait he uses to catch fish?
a) Fly
b) Worm
c) Flycatchers

8) If buccal is of the mouth what is adoral?
a) Of the heart
b) Near the mouth
c) Over the eye

9) What part of the body do these compartments apply to: rumen, reticulum, omasum, abomasum?
a) The brain
b) The stomach
c) The lungs

10) What does the word Ecology mean?
a) The study of an organism's relationship with its surroundings
b) The study of the complete habitat of a chosen area
c) The study of the relationship with an animal with the weather

11) What does the word feral mean?
a) One that has escaped from domestication and become wild

b) Night stalker
c) Carnivorous

12) Desert dwelling animals are often isabelline. What does that mean?
a) Light brown in colour
b) Thick-skinned
c) Web-footed

13) Most mammals are viviparous. What does that mean?
a) They have more than one colour on their coats
b) They give birth to live young
c) They have hair

14) Placental or true mammals are also called Eutheria. Why?
a) To indicate their position at the summit of the animal kingdom
b) To indicate the evolution of the placenta
c) To indicate the ability to move both on land and water

15) What is the term used when referring to the back of an animal?
a) Ventral
b) Dorsal
c) Cerval

16) What is Albumen?
a) It is a subfamily of white herring
b) It is the protein white of egg
c) It is the white crest of Asian domestic fowl

17) What is Amnion?
a) The fluid-filled sac in which the embryo develops

b) A small mountain bird
c) The young of an animal born in a zoo

18) What is Benthos?
a) It is the collective term for the family of whales
b) It is the collective term for animals and plants living at the bottom of the water
c) It is the collective term for large-horned ungulates

19) What does the term Poikilothermic or cold-blooded mean?
a) Creatures whose blood temperature is much lower than warm-blooded ones
b) Creatures whose body temperature varies with that of the surroundings
c) Creatures whose temperature is 0 degree Fahrenheit

20) What is Biology?
a) The study of animal life
b) The study of living organisms
c) The study of the relationship between animal and man

21) What is Bioluminescence?
a) The production of light by living organisms
b) The use of light as a prey-catching device by animals
c) The study of insects that are attracted by light

22) What is Blubber?
a) The exposed underbelly of the cat family
b) The soft upper layer of the palate of an aquatic animal
c) The fatty layer found below the dermis in aquatic animals

23) What is the soft-bodied larvae of moths and butterflies called?

a) Cassid
b) Caterpillar
c) Worm

24) What is an Ectoparasite?
a) An animal that lives as a parasite on the outside of another animal
b) An animal that lives off the insects found in the hair of another animal
c) An animal that lives as a parasite on the ectoplasma of humans

25) What does the scientific term 'F1' mean?
a) The primal theory of the origin of man
b) The first generation resulting from the cross between two parents
c) The primary food source of an animal

26) What does the scientific term 'F2' mean?
a) Progeny resulting from mating individuals of the F1 generation with each other
b) The secondary food source of an animal
c) The secondary theories about the origin of man

27) What is a Flagellum?
a) The thread that projects from a one-celled micro-organism which is used for motility
b) A parasite of the amoeba
c) The whip-like rod that hangs over the head of the angler fish

28) What is a Gonad?
a) An extinct member of the dwarf antelope species
b) A hermaphroditic insect
c) The reproductive organ of animals producing both sex cells and sometimes hormones

29) What is a Hyperparasite?
a) A worm that attacks another worm
b) An organism that lives as a parasite on another parasite
c) An animal that feigns sickness and is fed by the prey
hunted by the rest of the tribe

30) What is an Imago?
a) The adult stage of an insect
b) The imitation of sound by one species of another
c) The larval stage of a flea

31) What is the name of the protein that forms hair,
feathers, nails, claws, hooves and the outermost layer
of skin of vertebrates?
a) Frescatin
b) Terratin
c) Keratin

32) What is Limnology?
a) The study of fresh water and the animal and plant life
inhabiting it
b) The study of the effect of toxic wastes on mutating
aquatic species
c) The study of salt water insects

33) What is Morphology?
a) The study of dead animal tissue
b) The study of the effect of drugs on animals
c) The study of the form of living organisms

34) If nasal means 'of the nose', what does buccal mean?
a) Of the mouth
b) Of the stomach
c) Of the ear

35) What is Sericulture?
a) The raising of silkworms for the production of silk
b) The study of amoeba under the microscope
c) The artificial culturing of animal tissue to determine diseases

36) What is a Vivarium?
a) An enclosure for tropical butterflies
b) A place where animals are kept in conditions simulating their natural state
c) A snake zoo

37) What are Nektons?
a) Animals that actively swim in the upper part of the water
b) Animals that live off plankton exclusively
c) Freshwater plankton

38) When can a marine animal be described as oceanic?
a) When it lives where the water is more than 100 fathoms deep
b) When it lives exclusively in the ocean
c) When it can only survive in salt water

39) What is Pisciculture?
a) The study of animal urine used in tracking
b) The breeding of fish by artificial means
c) The destruction of lice from a given habitat

40) What is Parthenogenesis?
a) The development of ovum without fertilization
b) The creation of a second creature by splitting the first one
c) The regrowth of a severed limb

41) Where will you find a Phalange?
a) It is a bone of the finger/toe
b) It is a warm-blooded fish
c) It is a marsupial animal

42) What does Warning Colouration mean?
a) Animals and insects which have a conspicuous display
    of colour to advertise that they are either poisonous or
    discharge nauseous fluids
b) The change of colour by an animal or insect when
    under threat
c) The change of colour to advertise the coming change of
    season from hot to cold

43) Which creature's fighting habits have led to the phrase
    'pecking order' for social hierarchy?
a) The Domestic Fowl
b) The Domestic Turkey
c) The Coot

44) What, in ecological language, is a Quadrat?
a) The upper half of a rodent forehead
b) A piece of land marked off for the study of plants and
    animals
c) A coin with the depiction of an animal on it.

45) What is a Living Fossil?
a) A type of creature that has remained unchanged for
    hundreds of millions of years
b) A direct descendant of a dinosaur
c) A creature that has no active limbs

46) What is Apiculture?
a) The breeding of parakeets for commercial purposes

b) Beekeeping for the commercial sale of honey
c) The study of apes in an artificial habitat

47) What is a Terrarium?
a) A vivarium for land animals
b) A zoo for terrapins
c) An enclosure for crocodiles and alligators

48) What is Herpetology?
a) The study of anal diseases in primates
b) The study of bloodborne diseases in birds
c) The study of snakes and amphibians

49) What is Conchology?
a) The science of underwater sound
b) The study of natural birth control among insects
c) The science of the shells of molluscs

50) What is Taxidermy?
a) The art of preserving, stuffing and mounting animals in lifelike form
b) The transportation of animals to zoos
c) The migratory pattern of seabirds

51) What is Entomology?
a) The science of insects
b) The science of animal remains
c) The study of enteric diseases

52) What is Helminthology?
a) The study of bird beaks
b) The science of aquatic mammal migration
c) The study of parasitic worms

53) Crabs, lobsters, lizards, and crayfish have autotamy in common. What does that mean for them?
a) They can propel themselves with their tails
b) They can break off their limbs at will and regenerate the lost parts
c) They can change colour when threatened

54) What is a Wader?
a) An aquatic/riverside insect
b) An aquatic/riverside bird
c) A webfooted frog

55) What is the dropping and replacement of feathers called?
a) Redressing
b) Shedding
c) Moulting

56) What is the most common mating system in the animal kingdom?
a) Monogamy
b) Polygamy
c) Polygyny
d) Polyandry

57) Some animals sleep throughout the summer in the dry areas of the world. What is this called?
a) Aestivation
b) Hibernation
c) Maturation

58) What do farmers mean when they talk of biological control?
a) The use of pesticides to control pests

b) The use of pests' natural enemies to keep them under control
c) The use of natural fertilizers for the crops

59) What is Symbiosis?
a) A close association between two organisms to their mutual benefit
b) The search for new classifications
c) The process of assimilation in a lower order of mammals

60) What is Vacuum Behaviour in an animal?
a) When the animal responds in a genetically programmed manner in the absence of appropriate stimuli
b) The ability of an animal to survive when placed in a total vacuum
c) The behaviour of an animal in conditions of confinement

61) Ornithophily is common in the tropics but virtually absent in the temperate zone. What is it?
a) Flower pollination by birds
b) Migration from cold to hot zones by birds
c) Carnivorous behaviour by birds

62) Some animals sleep in winter when it is cold and food is unavailable. What is this sleep called?
a) Osomination
b) Hibernation
c) Parturition

1. a	2. b	3. a	4. a	5. c	6. a
7. a	8. b	9. b	10. a	11. a	12. a
13. b	14. a	15. b	16. b	17. a	18. b
19. b	20. b	21. a	22. c	23. b	24. a
25. a	26. a	27. a	28. c	29. b	30. a
31. c	32. a	33. c	34. a	35. a	36. b
37. a	38. a	39. b	40. a	41. a	42. a
43. a	44. b	45. a	46. b	47. a	48. c
49. c	50. a	51. a	52. c	53. b	54. b
55. c	56. c	57. a	58. b	59. a	60. a
61. a	62. b				

8

HAPPY FAMILIES

1)What is the Sea Anemone?
a) A comb jellyfish of the Coelenterata kingdom
b) A single-celled parasite of the hermit crab
c) A bootlace worm

2) What is the Indian Pangolin?
a) A wild cat of the Felidae family
b) A scaly anteater of the Myrmecophagidae family
c) A porcupine of the Hystricidae family

3) What is a Wildebeeste?
a) A general term used for wild animals
a) A gnu of the subfamily Antilopinae
c) A free ranging mountain goat of the Capra family

4) To which subfamily does the Grysbok (*Nototragus melanotis*) belong?
a) Dwarf Antelope
b) Wild Oxen
c) True Deer

5) What is the Chinese or Oriental Water Dragon?
a) A crested lizard
a) A giant salamander
c) A carnivorous fish

6) In which family of creatures does the female have bundles of hair on her abdomen which serve to diffuse attractant substances to the male?
a) Butterflies and moths (Lepidoptera)
b) Deer (Cervidae)
c) Loris (Loridae)

7) What is a Prairie Dog (*Cynomys ludovicianus*)?
a) A Wild Dog
b) A River Otter
c) A Squirrel Rodent

8) What is a Mannikin?
a) A bird of the Estrildidae family
b) A fish of the Agonidae family
c) The young of the Aye-aye Monkey of the Daubentoniidae family

9) To what breed of creature do these belong -- Lion's head, Little Red Riding Hood, Bugeye, Bouquet head, Sky Gazer?
a) Silverfish
b) Goldfish
c) Titi monkeys

10) What is a Colugo?
a) A flying lemur of the Cynocephalidae family
b) A squirrel like rodent of the Sciurmorpha family
c) A short-nosed fruit bat of the Cynopterinae family

11) What are a Purple Hairstreak, Ringlet and a Small Tortoiseshell?
a) Butterflies
b) Turtles
c) Terrapins

12) What is an Ocelot?
a) A member of the cat family
b) A member of the otter family
c) A baby ostrich

13) Which harmless animal, the size of a rabbit, without a tail, with a short snout and rounded ears is a close relative of the elephant?
a) The Hyrax (Hyracoidea)
b) The Tenrec (Tenrecidae)
c) The Uakari (Cebidae)

14) What are Burnished Brass, a Silver-Y, a Ghost Swift?
a) Cockle shells
b) Harlequin bugs
c) Moths

15) Which breed of domestic animal do these refer to -- Poitou, Spanish Giant, Savoy, Macedonian, Muscat?
a) Horse
b) Ass
c) Rooster

16) What are these – Queens Helmet, Strawberry Top, Lion's Paw, Miraculous Thatcheria and Sundial?
a) Types of small prawns found in plankton
b) Types of coral formations
c) Mollusk shells

17) Which creature has these types – mute, whooper, trumpeter, whistling?
a) White swans
b) Trout
c) Black geese

18) What are Seawasps (*Chironex fleckeri*)
a) Jellyfish
b) Shrimps
c) Woodlice

19) What is the Southern Polar Skua?
a) A relation of the Polar Bear of the Thalarctos genus
b) A seabird of the Stercorariidae family
c) A sea slug of the Cephalaspidae order

20) To what family does the Alpine Chough belong?
a) To the deer family of Cervidae
b) To the crow family of Corvidae
c) To the cuckoo family of Cuculidae

21) What is the Aadvark?
a) A large burrowing animal of the Orycteropidae family
b) A peccary of the Tayassuidae family
c) An anteater of the Mmyrmecophagidae family

22) What is a Sea Cow?
a) An aquatic mammal of the Sirenian order

b) A six-gilled shark of the Selachimorpha order
c) A right whale of the Cetacea order

23) What are Red Admirals and Dingy Skippers?
a) Cold water fish
b) Butterflies
c) River Crabs

24) Which members of the animal kingdom are the closest relatives of our reptile ancestors?
a) Amphibians
b) Birds
c) Fish

25) Which is the closest blood relative of the Earless Seals and the Sea Lions?
a) Bear
b) Shark
c) Octopus

26) What is a Lime Hawk, a Small Elephant Hawk, a Garden Tiger and a Green Carpet?
a) Crayfish
b) Snails
c) Moths

27) What breed of animals are the Kathiawari, the Marwari and the Manipuri?
a) Horses
b) Donkeys
c) Sheep

28) Which animal family is divided into red-toothed and white-toothed?
a) Marmoset

b) Wild Boar
c) Shrew

29) What are Terrapins?
a) Aquatic reptiles of the Emydidae family
b) Land mammals of the Edentata order
c) Non-flying birds of the Casuariformes order

30) What is an Ounce?
a) A term of weight of small animals
b) Snow leopard
c) It is the smallest Old World monkey

31) What is a *Panthera tigris?*
a) Panther
b) Tiger
c) Leopard

32) What is a Linsang?
a) Civet
b) Gibbon
c) Tree Shrew

33) Which animal is the closest relation of a cat?
a) Civet
b) Bandicoot
c) Otter

34) To what family does the Flying Fox belong?
a) Fox
b) Bat
c) Squirrel

35) Of which family is the Caracal a member?
a) Goat

b) Cat
c) Buffalo

36) To which family of animals does the Glutton (*Gulo gulo*) belong?
a) It is a member of the Weasel family
b) It is a type of Gorilla
c) It is an African Vulture

37) Which family do Civets belong to?
a) Tayassuidae
b) Mustelidae
c) Viverridae

38) To what species of animal do the Brussels Griffon, Rottweiler, Papillon, Borzoi, Chihuahua and Chow Chow belong?
a) Butterfly
b) Dog
c) Rat

39) Of what family is the Nilgai or Blue Cow (*Boselphagus tragocamelus*) a member?
a) Antelope (Tragocerinae)
b) Deer (Cervidae)
c) Oxen (Bovidae)

40) To which species do Bandicoots and Rat Opossums belong?
a) Even-toed Ungulates
b) Marsupials
c) Rodents

41) Which order do Cockroaches belong to?
a) Embioptera

b) Dictyoptera
c) Isoptera

42) To what breed do these creatures belong: Abyssinian, Bombay, Himalayan, Russian Blue?
a) Cat
b) Goat
c) Bear

43) To what group of animals does the Zorilla belong?
a) Striped Polecat of the Mustelidae
b) Anteater of the Myrmecophagidae
c) Pika of the Ochotonidae

44) Which are the closest relatives of the beautiful Yellow-Throated Marten of the Himalayas?
a) Otters, weasels, polecats (Mustelinidae)
b) Pheasants (Phasianidae)
c) Lemurs (Lemuridae)

45) Which of these creatures have a subfamily that can fly/parachute/glide from tree to tree?
a) Frogs
b) Snakes
c) Squirrels
d) Lizards
e) Apes
f) Monkeys

46) To what family does the Okapi belong?
a) Giraffidae
b) Cervidae
c) Camelidae

47) To which subfamily do the Suni, the Dik-dik, the Rhebok and the Klipspringer belong?
a) Dwarf Antelope (Neotraginae)
b) Sheep, Goats, and Goat-antelopes (Caprinae)
c) The True Antelopes (Antilopinae)

48) What is a Wolverine?
a) A female wolf
b) A member of the weasel and marten family
c) A member of the cat family

49) What creature is the Bombay Duck (Harpondon)?
a) An Eiderduck
b) A Waterbeetle
c) A Lantern fish

50) What is the Sea Cucumber?
a) Marine animal (*Pentacta tuberculosa*)
b) Fish (*Engraulis encrasicolus*)
c) Land animal (*Cyclopes didactylus*)

51) What animal is a Wobbegong?
a) A Shark of the Elasmobranchii subclass
b) A Ring-Tailed Cat of the Procyonidae family
c) A Panda of the Ailuridae family

52) What is known as the Laughing Jackass?
a) The Kookaburra Kingfisher (*Dactelo novaequineae*)
b) The Laughing Hyena (*Crocuta crocuta*)
c) The African Wild Ass (*Equus asimus*)

53) To what family do the Tuco-Tuco and Hutia belong?
a) They are Cavies of the Cavioidea family
b) They are Woodpeckers of the Picidae family
c) They are Cuckoos of the Cuculidae family

54) By what general name are the Serow, Goral and Takin better known?
a) Wild Oxen
b) Goat-antelopes
c) Domestic pigs

55) To what family of mammals does the Tasmanian Devil belong?
a) Ruminant
b) Carnivore
c) Marsupial

56) Of what family is the Shon a member of?
a) Deer (Cervidae)
b) Chevrotain (Tragulidae)
c) Walrus (Odobenidae)

57) To which group of animals does the Binturong of Assam and Sikkim belong?
a) Raccoon (Procyonidae)
b) Civet (Vivirreridae)
c) Bear (Ursidae)

58) What is a Pinniped?
a) An aquatic mammal with four limbs
b) An aquatic mammal with fins
c) A terrestrial amphibian

ANSWERS

1. a	2. b	3. b	4. a	5. a	6. a
7. c	8. a	9. b	10. a	11. a	12. a
13. a	14. c	15. b	16. c	17. a	18. a
19. b	20. b	21. a	22. a	23. b	24. b
25. a	26. c	27. a	28. c	29. a	30. b

31.	b	32.	a	33.	a	34.	b	35.	b	36.	a
37.	c	38.	b	39.	a	40.	b	41.	b	42.	a
43.	a	44.	a	45.	abcd	46.	a	47.	a	48.	b
49.	c	50.	a	51.	a	52.	a	53.	a	54.	b
55.	c	56.	a	57.	b	58.	a						

9
MONKEY BUSINESS

1) The most beautiful and the rarest of the Langur family, the Golden Langur, was only recently discovered. Where was it found?
a) Thimphu
b) Bali
c) Assam

2) Why is the Proboscis Monkey (*Nasalis larvatus*) so called?
a) It has a swollen, long, pendulous nose
b) Its sense of smell is the highest developed among monkeys
c) It has a vivid red nose which stands out in an otherwise dull brown body

3) What is the colour of the common Rhesus Monkey's face?
a) Jet Black
b) Livid Pink
c) Light Brown

4) Which monkeys are exported from India for vivisection and the testing of new drugs and -- as a result of that, borders on the endangered species list?
a) Spider monkeys (Atelinae)

82

b) Macaque monkeys (Macaca)
c) Howler monkeys (Alouattinae)

5) Which is the largest of the Gibbon family and where is it found?
a) The Siamang (*Hylobates syndactylus*) found in Malaysia and Sumatra
b) The Concolor Gibbon (*Hylobates concolor*) found in Vietnam, Indo-China and Southern China
c) The Kloss Gibbon (*Hylobates klossi*) of Sumatra

6) Which primate was Hollywood's King Kong?
a) The Mandrill (*Papio sphinx*)
b) The Orangutan (*Pongo pygmaeus*)
c) The Gorilla (*Gorilla gorilla*)

7) Which is the only ape found in India?
a) The Concolor Gibbon (*Hylobates concolor*)
b) The Hoolock's Gibbon (*Hylobates hoolock*)
c) The Pygmy Chimpanzee (*Pan paniscus*)

8) Which is commonest monkey of India?
a) The Rhesus Macaque (*Macaca mulatta*)
b) The Black Howler Monkey (*Alouatta carava*)
c) The White Collared Titi (*Callicebus torquatus*)

9) Which monkey is known as the Hanuman Monkey?
a) The Common Langur (*Presbytis entellus*)
b) The Emperor Tamarin (*Saguinus imperator*)
c) The Nilgiri Langur (*Presbytis johnii*)

10) Where do Baboons, Macaques and Lemurs store their extra food?
a) In the hollow of trees

b) In a large pouch in their cheeks
c) In an extra chamber of their stomachs

11) Where does a Langur store his extra food?
a) In the hollow of trees
b) In a hole in the ground covered with leaves and branches
c) In a special pouched chamber in the stomach

12) What distinguishes a Lemur from any other primate?
a) Its second toe has a claw rather than the flat nails of the other digits
b) Its tail is twice the size of its body
c) It has a musk pouch under its tail

13) What are the differences between New and Old World monkeys?
a) The thumbs of New World monkeys are usually atrophied
b) The tails of New World monkeys are usually prehensile
c) The New World monkeys usually have no tails
d) New World monkeys are duller, gentler, and easily tamed

14) Which primate has the most highly developed brain?
a) The Barbary Ape (*Macaca inua*)
b) The Sacred Baboon (*Papio hamadryas*)
c) The Chimpanzee (*Pan troglodytes*)

15) Which are the largest of the New World Monkeys?
a) Howler Monkeys (Ateles)
b) Woolly Monkeys (Lagothrix)
c) Owl-faced Monkeys (Aotes)

16) What colour are the cheeks of a Mandrill Baboon (*Mandrillus aphinx*)?

a) Bright green
b) Bright blue
c) Bright purple

17) What is the diet of a Gorilla?
a) Exclusively carnivore
b) Insectivore
c) Strictly vegetarian

18) The Sifakas, Indris and Avahis form the family of Indriidae. What are they characterized by?
a) They are tailless
b) They have only 30 teeth
c) They have the thickest fur of all the monkeys

19) What do all the Old World Monkeys have in common?
a) A well-developed thumb
b) Bare and highly coloured buttock patches
c) No more than two are born in a litter
d) Non-vegetarian in diet
e) Undeveloped thumbs

20) What is special about the Red Howler Monkey (*Atouatta seniculus*)
a) Its coat changes colour from red to orange and yellow
b) It is the only monkey that lives above a height of 8000 feet
c) Its call sounds like the variations of a trumpet

ANSWERS

1. c	2. a	3. b	4. b	5. a	6. c
7. b	8. a	9. a	10. b	11. c	12. a
13. abd	14. c	15. a	16. b	17. c	18. b
19. abc	20. a				

10
MAMMALS

1) Among the higher mammals which is the only creature which is completely airborne?
a) The Flying Lemur
b) The Bat
c) The Flying Squirrel

2) The Pikas (Ochotonidae) are members of the rabbit and hare order. In what way do they differ?
a) They are found in the mountains
b) They do not hibernate
c) They are larger than both rabbits and hares
d) They are mute

3) What is an elephant's tusk?
a) A modified incisor
b) An enlarged canine
c) An inverted horn

4) What is the main food of the Long-Tongued Bats (Macroglossidae) of the Indo-Malayan-Australian area?
a) Fruit
b) Nectar
c) Mice

5) Which of these are classified under the hound species of dog?
a) Dachshund
b) Beagle
c) Whippet
d) Bloodhound

e) Cocker Spaniel
f) Dalmatian

6) Which of these bovines is suited to both desert and mountain climates?
a) Bison
b) Gaur
c) Yak
d) Gayal

7) The Paraguayan Fox's (*Dusicyon gymnocercus*) diet, besides frogs, lizards, fishes, birds , and insects includes an unusual item. What is it?
a) Sugarcane juice
b) Vipers
c) Sheepskins

8) Which of these statements are true?
a) Elephants are superb swimmers
b) The African and the Indian elephant are closely related
c) Elephants walk very lightly, hardly leaving any tracks
d) Elephants sleep for most of the day

9) What is the condition of elephants known as musth?
a) The coming into oestrus of a female elephant
b) The secretion of a facial gland which causes aggression in male elephants
c) The inability to be tamed

10) Which is the largest terrier breed?
a) Airedale Terrier
b) Lakeland Terrier
c) Kerry Blue Terrier

11) How many times a year does a female dog come into oestrus or heat?
a) Once
b) Twice
c) Every forty days

12) Which is the largest Asiatic Wild Ass?
a) The Dzeggetai of Mongolia
b) The Kiang of Tibet
c) The Khur of India

13) Which was domesticated first?
a) Ass
b) Horse

14) The Hippopotamus (*Hippopotamus amphibius*) herds mark out their aquatic territories and defend them. Who is the head of the herd?
a) Male
b) Female
c) There are no heads of herds in this species

15) What is the difference between a Moose and an Elk?
a) None. What is known as moose in America is called elk in Europe
b) The moose is a member of the Deer family. The elk is a member of the Antelope family
c) The young of a moose is called an elk

16) The Caribou (*Rangifer tarandus*) of North America are distinguished from all other species of deer in one way. What is it?
a) They have an odd number of toes
b) Both the male and female grow antlers
c) They are the only deer to live off cave lichen

17) What is the main species of cattle you find roaming the streets of Indian cities?
a) Desi
b) Brahmany
c) Zebu

18) One of the well-known car names was Impala. What animal is an Impala?
a) Antelope (*Aepyceros melampus*)
b) Horse (*Equus impalayanus*)
c) Eagle (*Impalatus isidori*)

19) What is a cross between a stallion and a female ass called?
a) A cross is not possible
b) A Hinny
c) A Mule

20) The Tapir is a member of the odd-toed ungulate order which includes the horse and the rhinoceros. But it is different. How?
a) It is not a cud-chewer
b) It has an even number of toes
c) It has got only one toe

21) The Giant Armadillo (*Priodontes gigas*) is in the Edentata order but this seems to be inaccurately applied to it. Why?
a) It lays live young as well as eggs
b) It has no mammae
c) It has more teeth than any other mammal

22) A Jaguar is often mistaken for a Leopard. What are the differences?
a) The Jaguar is smaller than a leopard

b) The Jaguar's ring of spots has another spot inside it while the leopard's does not

c) A Jaguar's tail is shorter than a leopard's

23) All domestic cats are supposed to have evolved from which cat?
a) The Siamese Cat
b) The Caffre Cat
c) The Orinoco Cat

24) What do the Kinkajou (*Potos flavius*) of the raccoon family and the Binturong (*Arctitictis binturong*) of the civet family have in common?
a) They are the only two carnivores with prehensile tails
b) They are the only two carnivore family members who are vegetarian
c) They both change their colours according to the season

25) What is the peculiarity in the feeding habits of the North American Kangaroo Rat (*Dipodomys deserti*)?
a) It does not drink water
b) It eats a maximum of six times a year but hoards enormous quantities of food
c) It only eats desert lizards

26) How many teats are there on a cow's udder?
a) 4
b) 6
c) 8

27) Who are the parents of a mule?
a) Two mules
b) A female ass and a bull
c) A male ass and a mare

28) Where does a marsupial carry its young?
a) On its back
b) In its pouch
c) On its shoulders

29) What animal is known as the River Horse?
a) Walrus
b) Olingo
c) Hippopotamus

30) Which animal is the ancestor of the dog?
a) Wolf
b) Dhole
c) Dingo

31) What does a camel's hump contain?
a) Water
b) Fat
c) Protein

32) Which animal's burrow does the Hyena usurp and en-
    large for himself?
a) Porcupine
b) Fox
c) Mongoose

33) Palm Civets play a role in the dispersal of seeds. They
    ingest a fruit and the seed of that fruit is scattered in
    their droppings. Which seed is it?
a) Coffee berry
b) Mango
c) Avocado

34) Bats have an exceptional need for food and a constant level of humidity and temperature. Why?
a) The pores of the skin are large and so a great amount of heat escapes
b) The skin area is out of proportion to the volume of the body so a great quantity of heat is lost
c) The acids in the stomach burn up food at a much faster rate than any other mammal using a great deal of heat in the process

35) Why do bats choose caves to retreat into?
a) They have to have uniform conditions of temperature
b) They live off the lichen found in the caves
c) They cannot bear light

36) Which bats are smaller in size?
a) Fruit eating bats
b) Carnivorous bats

37) What does a fruit bat eat?
a) Fruit skin
b) Fruit pulp
c) Fruit juice
d) Fruit seeds

38) Why do bats whose mouths have been closed artificially in experiments blunder about?
a) Because their cries are an echo apparatus which guide the bats
b) Because the organ of balance is in the mouth and only works when the mouth is open and exposed to air
c) Because their organ of smell is in their mouth and that is the primary sense used by bats to find their way about

39) What are the differences between the musk deer
    (*Moschus moschiferus*) and other deer?
a) It is hornless
b) It has a gall bladder
c) It has a musk gland beneath the male abdomen skin
d) It has special mobile feet
e) It has four curved horns
f) It has a hump on its back

40) How does the mother Pangolin (*Amanis crassicau-
    data*) carry her baby?
a) In a pouch on her stomach
b) On her tail
c) On her back

41) What colour is a newborn Gaur (*Bos gaurus*)?
a) Light golden yellow
b) Dark brown
c) Blue-black

42) What colour is an old Gaur?
a) Grey
b) Jet black
c) Dark brown

43) How tall is an average bull Yak (*Bos mutus*) at the
    shoulder?
a) Eight feet
b) Five feet six inches
c) Three feet five inches

44) Typical sheep have three scent glands -- one on their
    face just below the eye, one in the groin. Where is the
    third located?
a) Under their necks

b) Below the left front leg
c) Between the two main toes of the feet

45) Which traveller and adventurer has had a sheep named after him?
a) Genghis Khan
b) Marco Polo
c) Rudyard Kipling

46) In which of the four chambers of the stomach is a bovine's food digested?
a) The first
b) The second
c) The fourth

47) What is a favourite food of the Indian Porcupine *Hystrix indica*?
a) The seed of the Jamun fruit
b) The dropped horns of deer
c) Snails

48) What is the difference between a hare and a rabbit at birth?
a) Hares have tails at birth which gradually fall off. The rabbit is born tailless
b) Hares are born in the open. Rabbits are born underground
c) Hares are well-furred with open eyes. Rabbits are nearly naked and blind

49) How many pregnancies does an average Mole Rat (Bathyergidae) have in one year?
a) 4
b) 6.8
c) 11.3

50) Which rodent attacks the farm crops?
a) The Indian Gerbil (*Tatera indica*)
b) The Little Indian Field Mouse (*Mus booduga*)
c) The Striped Field Mouse (*Apodemus agrarius*)

51) What is distinctive about rodent teeth?
a) There is always an empty gap in the jaw between the front and back teeth
b) Their two front teeth are enlarged greatly and they have no molars
c) They have no canine teeth, the space being occupied by the two enlarged front teeth

52) What does the Horse, the Rhinoceros and the Tapir have in common?
a) They all have similar horns which in the horse and tapir have worn down and are now considered non-existent
b) They are all leaf eaters
c) They have hoofed toes with the weight on the third toe

53) Which creature's dung is characterized by hard white balls composed chiefly of crushed bone?
a) Owl
b) Hyena
c) Mountain Goat

54) It has been observed that when there is a serious shortage of food wolves and wild dogs develop a disease. Which is it?
a) Rabies
b) Mange
c) Rickets

55) Which fruit is a special favourite of the jackal?
a) Jackfruit
b) Ber
c) Jamun

56) Which is the dominant sense in bears?
a) Sight
b) Smell
c) Touch

57) Can bears swim?
a) Yes
b) No
c) Some bears can

58) How is a bear's walk described?
a) Digitigrade
b) Plantigrade
c) Unguligrade

59) What is the favourite insect food of a Sloth Bear?
a) Honey Bees
b) Termites
c) Tiger Beetles

60) Which is the only species of Bear found south of the equator?
a) The Spectacled Bear (*Tremarctos ornatus*)
b) The Sloth Bear (*Melursus ursinus*)
c) The Malayan Sun Bear (*Helarctos malayanus*)

61) What is the typical feature for which a hyena is famous?
a) Its laughter call

b) Its scavenging habit
c) Its pink faeces

62) Which one of these is a scavenger?
a) Genet
b) Wild Dog
c) Civet
d) Hyena
e) Badger

63) What is the young Clouded Leopard (*Neofelis nebulosa*) often mistaken for because of the similarity in colour and pattern?
a) The Marbled Cat (*Felis marmorata*)
b) The Puma (*Felis concolor*)
c) The Fishing Cat (*Felis viverrina*)

64) How many kinds of cat species are there in India?
a) 6
b) 15
c) 43

65) What purpose do the bristling whiskers of a cat serve?
a) They are sensory, tactile organs
b) They serve as food filters
c) They serve no purpose

66) How do cats walk?
a) On their soles
b) On their toes
c) Flatfooted

67) What are a mammal's distinguishing characteristics?
a) It has mammae for suckling its young

b) It has four legs
c) The lower jaw has a single bone and is directly hinged to the skull
d) It has live young instead of eggs
e) It has a diaphragm separating the heart and lungs from the stomach and intestine
f) It has hair

68) Which is the largest of all extant members of the bovine family?
a) The Indian Bison (*Bos gaurus*)
b) The Domestic Buffalo (*Bubalus arnee bubalus*)
c) The African Buffalo (*Syncerus caffer*)

69) How many humps does a Llama have?
a) None
b) One
c) Two

70) What food does the Giant Panda live on exclusively?
a) Celery
b) Silk moths
c) Bamboo shoots

71) Why do both canine and feline breeds eat grass?
a) To supplement the meat diet
b) As a laxative
c) To induce vomit

72) How many offspring and descendants can a healthy pair of rats theoretically produce in three years?
a) 330 million
b) 450.000
c) 10.000

73) What is the name of the earliest known horse?
a) Eohippus
b) Hyracotherus
c) Ophisaurus

74) Which is the smallest horse breed in the world?
a) The Camargue
b) The Falabella
c) The Haflinger

75) Which mammal's eye-lenses have no power of accommodation so that it has to move its head to focus?
a) The Camel
b) The Horse
c) The Aardwolf

76) Which animal has greater endurance as a runner?
a) Cheetah
b) Horse
c) Mountain Goat

77) What are the young of a mule called?
a) Yulecalf
b) Mules are sterile
c) Mulerfoal

78) Many nocturnal carnivores have a distinctive phenomenon called eyeshine. What is it and what causes it?
a) An enlarged pupil caused by having more cones than rods
b) A layer of tapetum which reflects light at night
c) A vertical narrowing of the pupils caused by the chemical nocturnum which acts on the eye in the absence of light

79) What food does the Koala Bear live on exclusively?
a) Earthworms
b) Honey
c) Eucalyptus leaves

80) Which is faster – a Jackal or a Rabbit?
a) Jackal
b) Rabbit
c) Both are equally fast

81) Which is faster – a domestic Pig or a Chicken?
a) Pig
b) Chicken
c) Both are equally fast

82) How many chambers does a cow's stomach have?
a) One
b) Four
c) Six

83) How many humps does a Dromedary have?
a) One
b) Two
c) None

84) Which members of the mammal family lay eggs?
a) The Spiny Anteaters (Tachyglossidae)
b) The Phalangers (Phalangeridae)
c) The Duck-Billed Platypus (Ornithorhynchidae)
d) The Armadillos (Dasypodidae)

85) Apart from the pouch, there is one more major difference between marsupials and more advanced placental animals. What is it?

a) Marsupial toes are all curved while the other placental animals have flat toes
b) Marsupials have only one full set of teeth throughout their lives while the other animals have two or more
c) Marsupials keep growing till they die while other animals stop at maturity.

86) The tribe of Lemmings is famous for one peculiarity. What is it?
a) They commit mass suicide at regular intervals by drowning
b) All the females of the group produce their litters simultaneously
c) The first litter is always composed of only males

87) Which is the largest living rodent of these?
a) The Beaver (*Castor fiber*)
b) The Desert Jerboa (*Jaculus jaculus*)
c) The Mongolian Marmot (*Marmota sibirica*)

88) What are the differences between Indian and African elephants?
a) The Indian elephant has smaller ears
b) The Indian elephant has no tail
c) The Indian elephant has a higher forehead
d) The Indian elephant has only one finger at the end of its trunk instead of two
e) The Indian elephant has larger feet

89) Which is the only member of the Cat family that cannot retract its claws?
a) The Serval (*Felis serval*)
b) The Cheetah (*Acinonyx jubatus*)
c) The Margay (*Felis wiedi*)

90) How many bones does a Giraffe have in its long neck?
a) 23
b) 7
c) 110

91) Which of these is longer lived?
a) Cat
b) Dog

92) Which mammal has the longest hair of all?
a) The Musk Ox (*Ovibos moschatus*)
b) The Yak (*Bos mutus*)
c) The Mountain Goat (*Oriamnos americanus*)

93) What peculiar characteristic do the Hippopotamus and the Tapir share?
a) They have four toes on the front feet and three on the hind feet
b) Though they live almost exclusively on land, they defecate in the water
c) They both have an enlarged proboscis

94) What colour is the urine of a Javan Rhinoceros (*Rhinoceros sondaicus*)?
a) Red
b) Yellow
c) Colourless

95) Which of these dogs are used by the police forces for patrolling and detection?
a) Labrador Retriever
b) Bull Terrier
c) Dobermann Pinscher
d) Irish Wolfhound
e) German Shepherd

96) What is the average pregnancy period of a female Dog?
a) 63 days
b) 110 days
c) 35 days

97) Which of these statements are untrue?
a) Sugar produces stomach upset in dogs
c) Dogs do not need to eat anything other than meat
b) Salt in dogfood causes gas in the intestine
d) Dogs eat grass as a supplement to meat
e) Dogs miss meals when they are not well

98) The Nine-Banded Armadillo (*Dasypus novemcinctus*) has a curious reproductive feature. What is it?
a) It gives birth once in five years only
b) It always has a litter of four of the same sex and exactly alike
c) The male children are always larger than the female

99) What are the differences between a Hare and a Wild Rabbit?
a) A rabbit is smaller and lighter
b) A rabbit is gregarious while a hare is solitary
c) The rabbit is a burrower while the hare nests overland
d) The ears of a rabbit are shorter
e) The hare has a greater capacity for running and jumping

100) To what order does the Chinchilla (*Chinchilla laniger*) belong?
a) Rodentia
b) Marsupalia
c) Primate
d) Ruminant

101) To what order does the Australian Eastern Native Cat (*Dasyurus quoll*) belong?
a) Insectivores
b) Carnivores
c) Marsupials

102) Why is India's Palm Civet so named?
a) Its coat has a glossy palm design on it
b) It has a great liking for fermented toddy
c) It lives in palm trees

103) How many known species of mammal are there?
a) 4230
b) 9800
c) 7516

104) Which order accounts for 42% of the mammal?
a) Rodents (Rodentia)
b) Hares, Rabbits and Pikas (Lagomorpha)
c) Pangolins (Pholidota)

105) Which order accounts for 23% of mammals?
a) Whales (Cetacea)
b) Bats (Chiroptera)
c) Anteaters, sloths and armadillos (Edentata)

106) What is the peculiarity of the Gangetic Dolphin?
a) It is mostly vegetarian
b) It is black all over and has no fins
c) It is blind

107) Which is the heaviest among these?
a) Lion
b) Panther
c) Tiger

108) The Golden Hamster, now a popular pet, was only discovered as a single family of 12 in 1930. In which country was this family found?
a) Spain
b) Syria
c) Argentina

109) Why doesn't a Musk Ox (*Ovibos moschatus*) freeze to death in the extreme north Tundra where it lives all year round?
a) It has extremely long hair over thick layers of fat
b) It spends most of its life in moss-filled caves
c) It has the highest temperature of all mammals

110) Which of the primates is the closest relation of man?
a) Gibbons
b) Chimpanzees
c) Orangutans

111) The American Kennel Club has introduced a new breed of dog called the Cockapu. What is its ancestry?
a) A mixture of Cockerspaniel and Poodle
b) A mixture of Corgi and Pomeranian
c) A mixture of Collie and Pointer

112) What recognized breed of dog comes from India?
a) The Afghan Hound
b) The Rampur Hound
c) The Basenji

113) In which country was the cat first domesticated?
a) Thailand
b) Egypt
c) China

114) **What is the difference between a Dolphin and a Porpoise?**
a)   Porpoises have blunt snouts while dolphins have beak-like snouts
b)   They both refer to the same animal
c)   Dolphins have pelvic fins while porpoises lack them

115) **What is the difference between antlers and horns?**
a)   Antlers are solid
b)   Antlers are shed and regrown each year
c)   Antlers are curved while horns are straight

116) **There are no true Rabbits in the Indian subcontinent. What we see is the Hare. Is this statement true?**
a)   Yes
b)   No

117) **What is the main difference between a Mouse and a Rat?**
a)   The mouse has an enlarged first molar which is bigger than the other two molars combined
b)   The mouse has a much longer and thinner tail than the rat
c)   The mouse cannot see at night while the rat is a nocturnal animal

118) **In which mammal tribe does only one female breed at a time, the others hunting and bringing back food for her and her young?**
a)   African Bush Squirrels
b)   Wild Dog or Dhole
c)   Rock Voles

119) **What animal looks like a cross between a Giraffe and a Zebra?**
a)   The Chilean Pudu (*Pudu pudu*)

b) The Vicuna (*Llama vicugna*)
c) The Okapi (*Okapia johnstoni*)

120) Why is the name Swamp Deer given to the Bara-singha?
a) The Barasingha are a muddy dark brown in colour
b) The Barasingha eat marshweeds only
c) The Barasingha live on marshland and are seldom out of water
d) The Barasingha eat marshweeds only

121) Which is the largest Indian deer?
a) The Sambar (*Cervus unicolor kerr*)
b) The Axis Deer (*Axis axis*)
c) The Barbary Stag (*Cervus elaphus barbarus*)

122) Carnivores are distinguished by carnassial teeth. Which ones are these?
a) The last upper jaw premolars and the first lower jaw molars
b) The elongated canine teeth
c) The second lower jaw molars

123) Put these rodents in order of size :
a) Capybara (*Hydrochoerus hydrochaeris*)
b) Beaver (*Castor fiber*)
c) Pacarana (*Dinomys branickii*)
d) Large Indian Gerbil (*Tatera indica*)
e) Cape Jumping Hare (*Pedetes caper*)
f) Deermouse (*Peromyscus maniculatus*)

ANSWERS

1. a	2. a	3. a	4. b	5. abcd
6. c	7. a	8. a	9. b	10. a
11. b	12. b	13. a	14. b	15. a
16. b	17. c	18. a	19. b	20. b
21. c	22. b	23. b	24. a	25. a
26. a	27. c	28. b	29. c	30. a
31. b	32. a	33. a	34. b	35. a
36. a	37. b	38. a	39. abcd	40. b
41. a	42. b	43. b	44. c	45. b
46. c	47. b	48. c	49. c	50. a
51. a	52. c	53. b	54. b	55. b
56. b	57. a	58. b	59. b	60. a
61. a	62. d	63. a	64. b	65. a
66. b	67. acef	68. a	69. a	70. c
71. c	72. a	73. a	74. b	75. b
76. b	77. b	78. b	79. c	80. c
81. a	82. b	83. a	84. cd	85. b
86. a	87. a	88. acd	89. b	90. b
91. a	92. a	93. b	94. a	95. ace
96. a	97. bcd	98. b	99. abcd	100. a
101. c	102. b	103. a	104. a	105. b
106. c	107. a	108. b	109. a	110. b
111. a	112. b	113. b	114. a	115. ab
116 a	117. a	118. b	119. c	120. c
121. a	122. a	123. abcdef		

11
BIRDS

1) The Magpie Lark (*Grallina cyanoleuca*) male and female form a faithful lifelong pair and use the same territory every year. Both defend this territory in a curious way. How?
a) Each defends it only against birds of its own sex
b) They throw balls of feces at intruders
c) They land on intruding birds with their feet

2) How does a baby bird break out of its shell?
a) It uses the egg tooth on its bill
b) It uses its saliva to dissolve the shell
c) The mother breaks the shell open for it

3) Which bird family has a symbiotic relationship with the giraffe?
a) The Ox-peckers (Buphaginae)
b) The Drongos (Dicruridae)
c) The Egrets (Ardeidae)

4) Which common Indian bird's call is 'Wet my lips'?
a) The Grey Partridge (*Francolinus pondicerianus*)
b) The Common Quail (*Coturnix coturnix*)
c) The Grey Junglefowl (*Gallus sonneratii*)

5) The King Vulture (*Sarcorhampus papa*) is different in its diet from other vultures. How?
a) It will not scavenge human refuse
b) It only eats dead reptiles
c) It also eats live creatures which it catches itself

6) Which of these birds can travel the longest without flapping its wings?
a) Andean Condor (*Vultur gryphus*)
b) The Black Vulture (*Coragyps atratus*)
c) The Cayenne Kite (*Leptodon cayanensis*)
d) The Whistling Hawk (*Haliastur sphenurus*)

7) Which one of these birds can be recognized by its prominent tail?
a) The Painted Snipe (*Rostratula benghalensis*)
b) The Whitebellied Tree Pie (*Dendocitta leucogastra*)
c) The Blacktailed Godwit (*Limosa limosa*)

8) What is the general colour effect of these birds -- the Pink-headed Duck, the male Purple Sunbird and the male Indian Robin?
a) Black
b) Red and White
c) Pink and Purple

9) The Flamingo (*Phoenicopterus roseus*) has a very curiously inverted beak. What is it used for?
a) To peck the legs of intruders
b) To scoop the mud bottom and strain the minute food particles through
c) To act as a pouch for uneaten fish

10) After pairing, the female incarcerates herself in the hollow of a tree using her droppings to plaster the entrance. She stays there till her young are two weeks old and then breaks down the wall by attacking it steadily with her beak. Which birds have this curious nesting habit?
a) Hoopoes

b) Hornbills
c) Corncrakes

11) What stimulates a bird to migrate?
a) The length of the day which acts on the maturing of its reproductive organs
b) The increasing cold for which it is not adequately protected
c) The longer night and the increase of nocturnal predators

12) How many times does an average House Sparrow bring food to its nest?
a) 5-10 times
b) 50-70 times
c) 220-260 times

13) What colour is the crest of a peahen?
a) Grey, white and brown
b) Brown, white and green
c) Blue, green and brown

14) Birds interact with crocodiles in various ways, especially the Common Sandpiper (*Tringa hypoleucos*) and the Spur-winged Plover. What do these birds do?
a) They warn the crocodile of approaching danger
b) They pick parasites from their bodies
c) They bring them fish
d) They stand guard over crocodile eggs till they are hatched

15) What is odd about the Kookaburra (*Darcels gigas*)?
a) It is a kingfisher that no longer fishes

b) It is a parrot whose tongue is fused to the bottom of its mouth
c) It is a woodpecker which fishes

16) What is special about a Woodpecker's tongue?
a) As soon as it catches its prey it rolls up seven times crushing it
b) It is straight and stiff with an adhesive attachment at the end
c) It is four times the length of the beak and has a barbed tip

17) Why are Ovenbirds (Furnarius) so called?
a) They can only be found in the desert
b) They build mud nests that are baked hard by the sun rays
c) Their body temperature is higher than all other birds

18) The female Lyrebird (*Menura superba*) has an unusual way of keeping her nest clean after her single chick hatches. What does she do?
a) She eats all the droppings
b) She carries all the droppings from the nest to the nearest stream
c) She puts them into the male's mouth and he deposits them outside the nest

19) In East Africa the Black, Lappet-faced, Griffon, Egyptian, and Hooded Vulture will often congregate over one carcase. But there is a strict order of feeding. What is it?
a) Black
b) Lappet-faced
c) Griffon

d) Egyptian
e) Hooded

20) The Secretary Bird (*Sagittarius serpentarius*) of prey of Africa has a strange method of catching its prey. What is it?
a) It runs swiftly, stamping on it with strong feet or hitting it
b) It lurks behind rocks nd jumbs on its prey
c) It hits its prey with pebbles carried in its mouth and while it is stunned, swallows it whole

21) The Malle (*Leipoa ocellata*) bird builds an underground compost heap nest of decaying vegetable matter to lay its eggs in. The eggs take 8 months to hatch and the male keeps adjusting the mound to keep the temperature constant. To what degree?
a) 33 degrees Centigrade
b) 47 degrees Centigrade
c) 21 degrees Centigrade

22) The Skuas are known as the pirates of the polar regions. Why?
a) They steal the eggs of other seabirds and eat them
b) They attack other birds and make them disgorge their food
c) They have brown markings round their eyes which give them a pirate-like appearance

23) Which is the largest member of the Parrot and Parakeet family?
a) The Palm Cockatoo (*Probisciger aterrismus*)
b) The Vulturine Parrot (*Psittrichas fulgidus*)
c) The Blue and Yellow Macaw (*Ara ararauna*)

24) Which are the largest birds of the New World?
a) The Common Rheas (*Rhea americana*)
b) The Emu (*Dromaius novaehollandiae*)
c) The Giant Crane (*Dyatryma phorhacus*)

25) The seabirds Storm Petrels are named after St.Peter. Why?
a) Their mating cries sound like 'jee-zus meigh-ree'
b) They are the best fish catchers in the bird kingdom
c) They can lower their feet to skim the water surface and thus appear to walk on water

26) Pelicans are fish-eating waterbirds. What is their feeding peculiarity?
a) Their large beak pouch can hold 2-3 times more than their stomach
b) They can dive to several times their own body-length and shoot up apparently quite dry with their mouths stuffed with several fish
c) Though the adult pelicans eat fish they do not feed their young with anything but earthworms which they dig up with their feet and beaks

27) The bird Shoebill (*Balaeniceps rex*) is one of evolution's most bizarre freaks. Why?
a) It has a small tail growing in its caudal region
b) Its bill is shaped like a shoe with the upper mandible moveable only
c) Its huge bill is so heavy that the bird has to rest it on its neck for most of the time

28) What does the Woodpecker Finch (*Camarhynchus pallidus*) use to extract grubs from holes?
a) Its long and narrow beak

114

b) A cactus spine
c) Its sharp hooked claws

29) Which bird's wings are used for swimming instead of flying?
a) Giant Fulmars
b) Penguins
c) Rheas

30) Why are the Barbet birds so named?
a) They have rictal bristles which form beards
b) They have large crests
c) They are only found in Barbados

31) What is remarkable about the Hawfinch (*Coccothrausts coccothrausts*)?
a) Its ability to crack cherry and olive stones
b) It only eats the fruit of the Hawthorn tree
c) It is the only finch that does not migrate in winter

32) The nest of this bird was used by children in Eastern Europe as slippers. Which bird is it?
a) The Penduline Tit (*Remiz pendulinus*)
b) The Siskin (*Carduelis spinus*)
c) Velvet-fronted Nuthatch (*Sitta frontalis*)

33) What do the Tailor birds (Orthotomus) use to sew their nest leaves together to form their nests?
a) Dried straw
b) Spider webs
c) Fresh grass

34) Birds have no teeth. Where is their food broken up before being digested?
a) In the gizzard

b) In the throat
c) In the stomach

35) Which bird can throw its voice, like a ventriloquist, to mislead attackers?
a) Grebes (Podicipediformes)
b) Bitterns (Ciconiiformes)
c) Cassowaries (Casuariformes)

36) Which group of birds coming to the edge of the water try to push each other off balance to be the first to fall in?
a) Pelicans (Pelecanidae)
b) Diving Petrels (Pelecanoididae)
c) Penguins (Spheniscidae)

37) Which bird can rotate its head a 180 degrees on either side?
a) The Owl (Strigidae)
b) The Roller (Coraciidae)
c) The Nightjar (Caprimulgidae)

38) Which bird was known by its physical characteristics as the camelbird?
a) The Canvasback Pochard (*Aythya valisneria*)
b) The Ostrich (*Struthio camelus*)
c) The Magnificent Frigate Bird (*Fregata magnificens*)

39) Which bird is venerated in India as a symbol of fidelity and family unity?
a) The Baya Weaver Bird (*Ploceus philippinus*)
b) The Crimson-headed Sarus (*Grus antigone*)
c) The Demoiselle Crane (*Anthropoides virgo*)

40) Which is considered the best songbird of India?
a) The Shama (*Copsychus malabaricus*)
b) The Indian Wren-Warbler (*Prinia subflava*)
c) Malabar Whistling Thrush (*Myiophonous horsfieldii*)

41) The Egyptian Vulture (*Neophron percnopterus*) eats the eggs of the ostrich. How does it open the hard shells?
a) It hits them with its hard beaks until they crack
b) It lifts the eggs in its beaks and throws them down on the ground while flying
c) It takes stones in its beaks and throws them on the egg till it cracks open

42) Which birds are known as flying jewels? Thousands of them were killed in the early part of this century and their feathers used for women's ornaments.
a) Hummingbirds (Trochilidae)
b) Pheasants (Phasianinae)
c) Parrots (Psittaciformes)

43) Which is the weakest sense of birds?
a) Taste
b) Hearing
c) Smell

44) Which is the tallest Indian bird?
a) The Sarus Crane (*Grus antigone*)
b) The Adjutant Stork (*Leptoptilos dubius*)
c) The Barheaded Goose (*Anser indicus*)

45) Which has the widest wingspan of all the Indian birds?
a) The Large Cuckoo-Shrike (*Coracina novaehollandiae*)

b) The Himalayan Bearded Vulture (Lammergeier)
c) Tawny Eagle (*Aquila rapax*)

46) Which is considered the best 'talker' among Indian birds?
a) The Brainfever bird (*Cuculus varius*)
b) The Quaker Babbler (*Alcippe poioicephala*)
c) The Hill Myna (*Gracula religiosa*)

47) Which of these is the most common bird in India?
a) The House Crow (*Corvus splendens*)
b) The House Sparrow (*Passer domesticus*)
c) The Screech Owl (*Tyto alba*)
d) The Grey Partridge (*Francolinus pondicerianus*)
e) The King Crow (*Dicrurus adsimilis*)

48) What is the name of the earliest known bird?
a) Anapsida
b) Archaeopteryx
c) Sauropterygia

49) Which is the only bird that can move both the upper and lower parts of its beaks?
a) Parrot
b) Vulture
c) Falcon

50) Birds recognize each other initially by one sense alone. Which is it?
a) Sight
b) Smell
c) Sound

51) The African Honeyguide bird (*Indicator indicator*)
loves honeywax but it cannot break the honeybee hive.
What does it do?
a) It pushes the branches of the tree till the hive falls and
breaks
b) It leads honey badgers to the hive
c) It pecks at the exterior, worrying the bees till they
abandon the hive

52) Of the two sexes of birds, one sex forms 95% of the
singers. Which one is it?
a) Male
b) Female

53) Which bird was known in the heyday of falconry as the
Lady's Hawk?
a) The Redheaded Merlin (*Falco chiquera*)
b) The Dark Chanting Goshawk (*Melierax metabates*)
c) The Shahin Falcon (*Falco peregrinus peregrinator*)

54) Why do Vultures roost at night with their bare necks
tucked into their wings?
a) To protect the most vulnerable part of their bodies
b) To minimize the loss of heat
c) To increase their sense of security
d) The underside of the wings are the softest part of the
body, being covered with down and this is conducive to
sleep

55) Why is the Shrike known as the Butcher Bird?
a) It kills far more than it can eat and leaves several prey
untouched after killing them
b) It maintains a larder of impaled prey for later con-
sumption
c) It distributes parts of its prey to other colony birds

56) Why is a Tree Duck so called?
a) It lives in tropical forest pools feeding on tree fruit and other vegetation
b) It nests on trees
c) Its plumage is green and white

57) Which bird was such an easy prey to hunters that the Chinese are said to have used them to warm their hands?
a) The Chinese Quail (*Coturnix chinensis*)
b) The Chinese Pond Heron (*Ardeola bacchus*)
c) The Chinese Little Bittern (*Ixobrychus sinensis*)

58) Why do Ostriches eat pebbles?
a) To help digestion by grinding up the ingested food
b) At nesting time they burrow the ground with their beaks and the pebbles are eaten during this clearing up
c) To obtain calcium

59) Which bird is regarded as the ancestor of all domestic poultry?
a) The Red Jungle Fowl (*Gallus gallus*)
b) The Green Jungle Fowl (*Gallus varius*)
c) The Javanese Woodcock (*Scolopax saturata*)

60) King Emperor Penguins have a unique way of incubating their eggs. What is it?
a) They breathe on them constantly to keep them warm
b) They hold them under their flippers till they hatch
c) They hold them off the cold ground between their feet

61) Which bird family sneaks its eggs into other birds' nests to hatch?
a) The True Cuckoo

b) The Raven
c) The Roadrunner

62) Why are birds' bones hollow?
a) To keep them light
b) To store extra food
c) To store inhaled air

63) The Lammergeyer Vulture (*Gypaetus barbatus*) of the Himalayas is different from other vultures. In what ways?
a) It captures live prey
b) It eats only bone and bone marrow
c) It supplements its carrion diet with grass and plants
d) It has feathers on its head and neck
e) It looks like an eagle

64) Which bird is called 'the falconer's dream' for its ability to hunt large animals as well?
a) The Prairie Falcon (*Falco mexicanus*)
b) The Golden Eagle (*Aquila chrysaetos*)
c) The Old World Kestrel (*Falco tinnunculus*)

65) The Indian bird *Acridotheres tristis* is such an efficient grasshopper-eater that it has been sent to Mauritius to control the grasshopper population there. Which bird is this?
a) The Cormorant
b) The Fairy Bluebird
c) The Common Myna

66) Owls have a curious eating habit. What is it?
a) They only eat in the dark

b) They ingest the whole prey and then cast up the indigestible part of their food in the form of pellets
c) They only attack moving prey

67) Birds have a special organ for producing voice, situated at the fork of the windpipe. What is this called?
a) Audior
b) Ortholarynx
c) Syrinx

68) Which bird was used by Indian police communication departments to communicate to remote outposts before radio came into general use?
a) Pigeon
b) Kite
c) Swallow

69) Which bird's call is the question 'Did you do it?'
a) The Sacred Ibis (*Threskiornis aethiopica*)
b) The Redwattled Lapwing (*Vanellus indicus*)
c) The Indian Openbill (*Anastomus oscitans*)

ANSWERS

1. a	2. a	3. a	4. b	5. a
6. a	7. b	8. a	9. b	10. b
11. a	12. c	13. b	14. a	15. a
16. c	17. b	18. b	19. abcde	20. a
21. a	22. b	23. c	24. a	25. c
26. a	27. c	28. b	29. b	30. a
31. a	32. a	33. b	34. a	35. a
36. c	37. a	38. b	39. b	40. a
41. c	42. a	43. c	44. a	45. b
46. c	47. a	48. b	49 a	50. c
51. b	52. a	53. a	54. a	55. b

56. a	57. a	58. a	59. a	60. c
61. a	62. ac	63. bde	64. b	65. c
66. b	67. c	68. a	69. b	

12
REPTILES

1) Does the Turtle discard and replace its shell once it outgrows it?
a) The shell is not a covering but part of its skeleton
b) The shell is discarded three times in an average turtle's lifetime
c) Some turtles living near the sea discard their shells while they fish for food. Land turtles never discard their shells

2) Where is a Rattlesnake's rattle?
a) At the tip of its tail
b) In its mouth
c) On its hood

3) What is unique about the Iguana family member – the Basilisk?
a) It never blinks and its eyes hypnotize prey larger than it
b) Not only does it run on land but also on large stretches of water
c) It never sheds its skin

4) How does the Gecko run over house walls or ceilings?
a) Its lamellate cushioned feet have microscopic hook cells which engage themselves in the tiniest irregularities of a surface

b) Its lamellate cushioned feet exert a suction on the surface

c) Its lamellate cushioned feet secrete a sticky substance that enables them to cling to smooth surfaces

5) The Tokay (*Gecko gecko*) is the best-known gecko of Asia. Its call 'geck-oh' or 'to-keh' is considered a sign of good luck in a house. But only one of the sexes has a voice. Which one is it?

a) Male

b) Female

6) What is special about the Crocodile's tongue?

a) It has fine teeth run along its edges

b) It is forked at the end

c) It is fused to the bottom of the mouth

7) The Snake has very few predators. Which animal of these is the main one?

a) Mongoose

b) Eagle

c) Wild Dog

8) Is the music played by snake charmers necessary for the Cobra to dance?

a) No. The snake is deaf and is responding to the threatening movement of the musical instrument

b) Yes. The snake is the most musical of the animal kingdom

c) The snake does not need the movement or the flute. When its hood is raised it always sways

9) What is the easiest way to distinguish between a Crocodile and an Alligator?

a) The alligator is black with a thin snout. The crocodile is dull brown with a thick snout

b) In the alligator the upper teeth cover the lower. In the crocodile a large lower tooth shows when the mouth is shut

c) The tail of the alligator is half the length of its body, whereas the crocodile's tail is the same size as its body

10) Which of these is a Hamadryad?
a) The Egyptian Cobra
b) The Banded Krait
c) The Spitting Cobra
d) The King Cobra

11) Which snakes are considered the most intelligent of extant snake groups?
a) The Rattle-bearing Pit Vipers (*Crotalus*)
b) The True Cobras (*Naja*)
c) The Puff Adders (*Bitis*)

12) When the baby Crocodile is ready to emerge from its nest under the sand how does it get out?
a) It cracks its egg and uses snout to burrow its way out of the sand
b) It chirps to its mother who digs the sand till the eggs are exposed and then cracks them

13) Why do the parent Crocodiles eat the eggs and membranes of the hatched baby crocodiles immediately?
a) To increase their calcium reserves
b) To avoid attracting predators
c) They regurgitate them into the mouth of the young as their first meal

14) Why are Pit Vipers so called?
a) They live in hollows and pits

b) They have pits between the nostril and eye which are heat sensitive so that warm-blooded prey can be located at night
c) Their skin is patterned in a light and dark way to suggest holes on it

15) How many living species of reptile are recorded?
a) 11,592
b) 5,175
c) 34,720

16) Which of these orders forms 94% of the total reptile population?
a) Squamata
b) Crocodilia
c) Rhynchocephalia
d) Chelonia

17) What is the curious feature of a snake's lungs?
a) The left lung is greatly reduced while the right is greatly enlarged
b) It has none
c) They are not parallel, but one below the other

18) Geckos, Agamas and Iguanas have a special grouping within the Squamata family of lizards and snakes. What are they known as?
a) Lizards with prehensile tails
b) Burrowing lizards
c) Lizards with thick tongues

19) Do Snakes have teeth?
a) Yes
b) No
c) Some snakes have teeth

20) The Viviparous Lizard (*Lacerta vivipara*) is remarkable among animals. Why?
a) It devours more than half its offspring immediately after their birth
b) It lays both eggs and bears live young
c) It sleeps with its head buried under the sand

21) Which harmless Snake in India, when provoked, turns over and plays dead?
a) The Common Cat Snake
b) The Common Blind Snake
c) The False Coral Snake

22) The Common Krait Snake is found all over the Indian subcontinent. But it is much less in the North-east where it is hunted and eaten by another predator. Which one?
a) The Banded Krait Snake (*Bungarus fasciatus*)
b) The Otter Civet (*Cynogal bennetti*)
c) The Black-footed Ferret (*Mustela nigripes*)

23) How has the Gecko adapted itself to walking over desert sand?
a) It only walks on the sand when it is cooler at night. During the day it stays in its burrow under it
b) It has developed footpads without any sensitivity to heat
c) It has developed webbed feet

24) What do the special cells called chromatophores do for the Chameleon?
a) They cause it to change colour
b) They cause it enlarge its neck-glands
c) They cause it to see better

25) When the size of the chromatophore cells enlarges, what effect does it have on the Chameleon?
a) There is more colour on the body
b) There is less colour on the body
c) It can see in the dark

26) Why is the large-scale killing of Cobras an ecological and agricultural disaster for India?
a) Cobras help in the cross-fertilization of certain edible seed plants
b) Cobras control the rodent population
c) Cobras are the main diet of certain birds which help in cross pollination

27) What is the difference in the eating habits of the Gharial (*Gavialis gangeticus*) to the other two crocodile species?
a) It eats twice a day
b) It is mainly vegetarian
c) It eats only fish

28) Which harmless, beneficial snake, often mistaken for a Cobra, growls when caught and inflates its body?
a) The Rat Snake (*Elaphe obsoleta*)
b) The Blunt-headed Tree Snake (*Inantodes cenchoa*)
c) The Western Hog-nosed Snake (*Heterodon nasicus*)

29) From which creatures have snakes evolved?
a) Armadillos
b) Lizards
c) Wormfish

30) When the Snake sheds its skin, which of these are also shed?
a) Eyecaps
b) Teeth

c) Fangs
d) Tongue-tips
e) Poison glands

31) Which is the only snake in the world that builds a nest?
a) Javelin Sand Boa (*Eryx jaculus*)
b) Green Vine Snake (*Oxybelis fulgidus*)
c) King Cobra (*Ophiophagus hannah*)

32) Which live animal is used to make anti-snake venom in the Haffkine Institute in Bombay?
a) Cow
b) Horse
c) Pig

33) Where did the largest prehistoric tortoise *Colossochelys atlas* live?
a) India
b) The Seychelles
c) China

34) Colubrid snakes have surprisingly often been found with a mutation. What is it?
a) With two heads that act independently
b) With teeth
c) With albino colouring

35) Which is the largest family of snakes?
a) The Python, Boa and Anaconda group of Boids
b) The Cobra and Sea snake group of Elapids
c) The Ringed and Smooth snake group of Colubrids

36) Where does the old skin of a snake first split when it is sloughing it off?
a) Round the lips
b) At the end of the tail
c) Over the eyes

1. a	2. a	3. b	4. a	5. a	6. c
7. a	8. a	9. b	10. b	11. a	12. b
13. b	14. b	15. b	16. a	17. a	18. c
19. a	20. b	21. a	22. a	23. c	24. a
25. a	26. b	27. c	28. a	29. b	30. abcd
31. c	32. b	33. a	34. a	35. a	36. a

13

A WORLD WITHIN A WORLD

1) How many wings does a flea have?
a) Four
b) Six
c) None

2) Why is a Stag Beetle *(Lucanus cervus)* so named?
a) The male mandibles have enlarged into hard antlers by which they fight each other
b) The males roam in packs with other males only
c) They are herbivorous

3) To which insect did the ancient Greeks sacrifice an ox every year at Actium in the hope it would not attack them?
a) The Common Housefly *(Musca domestica)*
b) The Sheep Louse *(Linognathus ovillus)*
c) The Paper Wasp *(Polistes canadensis)*

4) How many pairs of wings does a Butterfly have?
a) 2

b) 4
c) 6

5) How many eyes does a Housefly have?
a) Two simple eyes
b) Two compound eyes
c) Two simple and two compound eyes

6) Where does a Bee keep its sting?
a) In its proboscis
b) Just under its second pair of wings
c) Under its abdomen

7) What colours are Ladybirds?
a) Yellow and red
b) Yellow, red and black
c) Red and black

8) How many Queen Bees does one beehive have?
a) One
b) Two
c) Four

9) How many types or orders of insects are there?
a) 33
b) 42
c) 29

10) How does the Cricket produce its song?
a) Through its enlarged vocal sac called the hypopharynx
b) By scraping one part of the leg called the file against the front wing
c) By rubbing the hindwings together

11) How do fleas locomote?
a) Crawling
b) Jumping
c) Flying

12) What does the word Lepidoptera mean and which group of insect does it signify?
a) Hard wings. Beetles and weevils
b) Scale wings. Butterflies and moths
c) Fringe wings. Thrips

13) What is special about the saliva of bloodsucking insects?
a) It transmits a parasite to the host
b) It contains an anticoagulant
c) It contains an antihystamine

14) What is the principal food of the mosquito?
a) Human blood
b) Garbage
c) Plant nectar

15) Who discovered that mosquitoes were carriers of disease and which disease was first identified?
a) Dr. Stanley Livingston – Malaria
b) Sir Patrick Manson – Filariasis
c) Marie Curie – Typhus

16) The tempo of which insect's song can tell you the temperature in degrees Fahrenheit?
a) Cricket (Gryllidae)
b) Hornets (Vespinae)
c) Fireflies (Lampyridae)

17) After the egg comes the caterpillar and then the butterfly. What is the stage between egg and cicada?
a) Nymph
b) Larva
c) Spat

18) How many eyes does a cockroach have?
a) Two compound and three simple eyes
b) Four compound eyes
c) Two simple eyes

19) Which insect can stand 100 times the radiation that man can and is still normal at 126 gs of gravity while man can only take up to 18?
a) The Worker Honey Bee (Apis mellifera)
b) The Cockroach (Blattaria)
c) The Hercules Beetle (Dynastes titus)

20) Which insect causes the plague?
a) The Anopheles Mosquito (Anopheles bifurcatus)
b) The Oriental Rat Flea (Xenopsylla cheopis)
c) The Horsefly (Tabanus bovinus)

21) Which is the largest known lepidopteran?
a) The South American Owlet Moth (Thysania agrippine)
b) The Hawkmoth (Deilephila elpenor)
c) The Cabbage White Butterfly (Pieris brassicae)
d) The Hercules Emperor Moth (Coscinoscera hercules)

22) How does the Queen Bee know the difference between the worker and the drone eggs she lays?
a) By their smell
b) By the thickness of their shell
c) By their size

23) One family of insects takes two to three years to mature, but their adult lives are often less than a day. Which family is this?
a) Grasshoppers (Orthoptera)
b) Mayflies (Ephemeroptera)
c) Cicadas (Homoptera)

24) Which insects feign death on being attacke by bleeding from their knee joints?
a) Ladybird Beetles (Coccinellidae)
b) Pomace flies (Drosophilidae)
c) Dryinids (Dryinidae)

25) If an insect is brightly coloured and conspicuous in its normal surroundings, what can the rest of the animal world conclude?
a) It is poisonous and unfit to eat
b) It has migrated from some other surroundings and is not a native of the habitat in which it presently is
c) It can be eaten safely

26) What is Batesian mimicry in insects?
a) When a smaller insect copies a larger insect in colouring in order to gain access to its nest
b) When a harmless species copies a harmful one as a defence measure
c) When an insect exudes the same smell as another of a different species

27) What is Mullerian mimicry in insects?
a) When two harmful species share a common colour pattern
b) When the attack pattern of a harmful insect is copied by a harmless one
c) Similar colour patterns among the beetle species

28) In which species of insects does a food-carrying worker have to give a pass sign to the guard before it is allowed into the nest?
a) Bees
b) Ants
c) Termites

29) Formica Ants keep other creatures as herds, milk them, move them around, build shelters for them and supervise their grazing. Which creatures are these?
a) Aphids (Aphidae)
b) Round Carrion Beetles (Liodidae)
c) Primate Lice (Pediculidae)

30) Bees can only distinguish six colours. Which are they?
a) Ultraviolet
b) Infrared
c) Violet
d) Red
e) Bluish
f) Purple
g) Grey-white
h) Yellow
i) Blue
j) Black

31) What causes Locusts to migrate to new lands?
a) More interesting food
b) Overpopulation
c) The comparative rarity of predators in the new land

32) With what sense does the female Mosquito attract the male?
a) Sound
b) Sight
c) Smell

33) Which Butterfly has enough poison in its body to kill a medium-sized bird?
a) The Monarch Butterfly *(Danaus plexipus)*

b) The Privet Hawkmoth *(Sphinx ligustri)*
c) The Spanishfly *(Lytta vesicatoria)*

34) How many eggs does an average Queen Honeybee lay
    in a lifetime?
a) 1,500,000
b) 200,000
c) 40,000

35) Which tree leaves does the Silkmoth caterpillar *Bombyx
    mori* feed on?
a) Mango
b) Mulberry
c) Chinese jujube

36) One of the most common insects and a household eater
    of books is a living fossil. Which one of these is it?
a) Silverfish
b) Cockroach
c) Common Clothes Moth

37) What is the glow of a Firefly (Lampyridae) caused by?
a) The friction caused by the rubbing together of its
    wings
b) A substance called Luciferin in the organ on its abd-
    omen
c) The reflection of its compound eyes caused by eye-
    shine

38) Why is the glow of the Glowworm produced?
a) To attract a mate
b) To find its way in the dark
c) To warn off predators

39) Fleas were used for 'flea circuses' where they were made to jump through hoops, hold up small ballerina dolls and make them revolve. However only one sex of flea was used as the other was considered too weak to perform. Which was it?
a) Male
b) Female

40) How many legs does a Mite have?
a) Six
b) Four
c) Eight

41) Which insects swim upside down on their backs?
a) Water Striders (Gerridae)
b) Water Treaders (Mesoveliidae)
c) Water Boatmen (Corixidae)

42) What is the average lifespan of a Housefly?
a) 17 days
b) 45 days
c) 10 months

43) Which sex of Mosquito bites humans?
a) Male
b) Female
c) Both

44) The Death's Head Hawkmoth *(Acherontia atropos)* sometimes sneaks into a beehive unnoticed. How does it do that?
a) The underside of its wings have the same colouring as a bee so it raises its wings
b) By mimicking the piping sound of the queen bee
c) It covers itself with nectar

45) Several insect groups including bees and wasps are parasitized by an insect group called Stylops. What happens to females attacked by Stylops?
a) They are gradually debilitated and finally paralysed
b) They change in form to males
c) They die

46) Which of these animal species also get malaria from mosquito vectors?
a) Fowl
b) Monkeys
c) Pigs
d) Deer

47) Which fly is commonly found in slaughter houses?
a) The Greenbottle Fly *(Lucilia caesar)*
b) The House Fly *(Musca domestica)*
c) The Stable Fly *(Stomoxys calcitrans)*

48) What is the preferred diet of the Silverfish *(Lepisma saccharina)*?
a) Dead wood
b) Starch and sugar
c) Decayed plants

49) Which diseases do headlice *(Pediculus humanus capitis)* spread?
a) Relapsing fever
b) Typhus
c) Jaundice
d) Malaria
e) Elephantiasis

50) The Bee Killer Wasp *(Philanthus triangulum)* does not kill her prey but paralyses it, takes it to her tunnel, lays an egg on it which when hatched feeds off the live but paralysed prey provided for it. What prey is it?
a) The Bumblebee (Bombini)
b) The Honeybee (Apini)
c) The Stingless Bee (Meliponini)
d) The Carpenter Bee (Xylocopini)

51) Which carnivorous insects prey on other insects by imitating them right down to the smallest detail? They can even deceive human collectors who mistake them for a mosquito or a stick insect.
a) Shield bugs (Pentatomidae)
b) Ambush bugs (Phymatidae)
c) Assassin bugs (Reduviidae)

52) What are anabiotic insects?
a) Insects which survive cold spells by suspending their living activities
b) Insects which live in tropical zones
c) Insects which can walk backwards

53) When a Wasp colony is disturbed and is about to be abandoned, what do the wasps do first?
a) The workers destroy the drones
b) A small swarm escorts the queen out
c) They feed on the eggs and larvae

54) When a Bee returns to the hive, it performs a waggle and figure eight dance. What does the angle and tempo indicate?
a) The source and distance of the nectar it is carrying
b) The presence of predators
c) Whether or not it has found nectar

55) Which insects are important agents in the biological control of mosquitoes and flies?
a) Waterbeetles (Gyrinidae)
b) Dragonflies (Anisoptera)
c) White Flies (Aleyrodidae)

56) In China insect fights of these species are common, with a lot of betting involved. Which species is it?
a) Praying mantis *(Mantis religiosa)*
b) Hercules beetle *(Dynastes tityus)*
c) Cockchafer *(Melolontha melolontha)*

57) What is the role of Honeypot Ants in an ant colony?
a) They store the nutrient liquid tapped from aphids in their bellies
b) They are in charge of the stored honey in the honey-cells of the colony
c) They are in charge of feeding the queen ant

58) Which insect gives a local anaesthetic to its victim before it draws its blood?
a) The Biting Midge (Ceratopogonidae)
b) The Mosquito (Culicidae)
c) The Buffalo Gnat (Simuliidae)

59) Which insect colony has a king, a queen, soldiers, and workers?
a) Ant
b) Termite
c) Bee

60) What are the common diseases spread by flies?
a) Cholera
b) Leprosy
c) Paratyphoid

d) Typhoid
e) Yaws
f) Tuberculosis
g) Poliomyelitis
h) Rickets

61) How does an Antlion (Myrmeleonidae) catch its prey?
a) It digs a pit, crawls in and waits for an ant to fall in
b) It hides behind trees and springs on the deer's neck
c) It runs after the snake and seizes it by the back of the
   head

ANSWERS

1. c	2. a	3. a	4. a	5. b	6. c
7. c	8. a	9. c	10. b	11. b	12. b
13. b	14. c	15. b	16. a	17. a	18. a
19. b	20. b	21. d	22. c	23. b	24. a
25. a	26. b	27. a	28. b	29. a	30. acefhi
31. b	32. a	33. a	34. a	35. b	36. a
37. b	38. a	39. b	40. c	41. c	42. a
43. b	44. b	45. b	46. ab	47. a	48. b
49. ab	50. b	51. c	52. a	53. c	54. a
55. b	56. a	57. a	58. b	59. b	60. acdefg
61. a					

14
ARACHNIDS

1) Scorpions are mainly desert animals. What were their
   ancestors?
a) Marine animals

b) Tropical forest animals
c) Arctic animals

2) Which spiders can change the colour of their eyes?
a) Jumping Spider (Attids)
b) Water Spiders (Lycosids)
c) Orb Weavers (Argyopids)

3) One species of spider hunts fish, often going below the water to capture minnows. Which one is it?
a) Jumping Spiders *(Salticus scenicus)*
b) The Raft Spider *(Dolomedes fimbriatus)*
c) The Wolf Spider *(Pisaura mirabilis)*

4) What is the name of the organ on the spider's body from which silk is produced for the web?
a) Webster
b) Threadery
c) Spinneret

5) The Solpugida or Wind Scorpions are small (1-5 cm) but the most savage of all the arachnids, attacking small birds and lizards. Their huge jaws are unusual. How?
a) Though toothless the jaws are sharpened into powerful razors
b) They are paired and bite vertically
c) Once the scorpion clamps them on its prey they lock into place

6) How many legs has a Spider?
a) 8
b) 6
c) 4

7) Which are the only marine arachnids?
a) King Crabs *(Limulus polyphemus)*
b) Star Barnacle *(Chthamalus stellatus)*
c) Sea Whip *(Funicula quadrangularis)*

8) Why is an arachnid not an insect?
a) It has four eyes instead of two
b) It spins webs to catch its prey instead of a direct assault on its victim
c) It has 8 legs instead of 6

9) What is the difference between centipedes and millipedes
a) Centipedes have 100 legs and millipedes have 1,000 legs
b) Centipedes are much larger than millipedes
c) Centipedes have one pair of legs on each segment and millipedes have 2 pairs of legs on each segment

10) How do slugs and snails breathe?
a) Through their skin
b) Through their nostrils
c) Through a lung that opens out on the side of the body

11) Why are watersnails useful in an aquarium?
a) They keep down the growth of algae on the sides of the tank by eating it
b) They are live protein food for the fish
c) Their shells provide calcium to the fish

ANSWERS

1. a	2. a	3. a	4. b	5. c	6. b
7. a	8. c	9. c	10. c	11. c	

15
WHERE IT ALL BEGAN

1) How does a Chinese Liver Fluke enter man?
a) Through badly cooked pork
b) Through raw fish
c) Through oysters

2) Which animals does the tapeworm use as his hosts?
a) Pigs
b) Geese
c) Cattle
d) Fish
e) Cats

3) Which worms cause hookworm which, in turn, causes anaemia and mental backwardness?
a) Necator
b) Annelida
c) Kamtozoa

4) What is the skeleton of the earthworm called?
a) Conulata
b) Radiata
c) It does not have a skeleton

5) Which single-celled animal causes dysentery?
a) Chonotricha
b) Coelomata
c) Entamoeba

6) Which single-celled animal causes sleeping sickness and what is its vector?
a) Polymorphosone -- Culex mosquito

b) Trypanosome – Tsetse fly
c) Entodiniomorpha – Rat flea

7) Which single-celled animal causes malaria?
a) Cilia
b) Plasmodium
c) Balantidium

8) What is the horny outer covering of arthropods called?
a) Cuticle
b) Shell
c) Skeleton

9) What is a single-celled animal called?
a) Protozoa
b) Trypansoma
c) Amoeba

10) How does an Amoeba move?
a) It flows, pushing out pseudopodia in front and pulling in at the rear
b) Its flagella points backwards and deliver a pushing force
c) It does not move but floats in fresh or salt water

11) What are pseudopodia?
a) Adhesive tentacles that capture small organisms in the water
b) Small fingerlike projections of the amoeba
c) Calcereous platelets which are motile

12) From which creature is chalk made?
a) The shells of the unicelled Globigerina family
b) The calcareous sponge of the Pharetronida family

c) The skeleton of the compressed Comb Jellyfish of the Platyctenidea family

13) Which of these microbes are animals instead of vegetables?
a) Protozoa
b) Bacteria
c) Mycoplasma
d) Virus

14) How many teeth does the slug *Limax maximus* have on its flexible ribbon tongue?
a) 40,000
b) 28
c) 620

15) How do Earthworms tunnel through the earth?
a) By swallowing the soil as they burrow
b) By expanding and contracting their bodies
c) By secreting an acid which dissolves the soil

16) What happens when you cut a Flatworm in half?
a) It dies
b) Each half forms a new flatworm
c) It changes colour before it dies

17) How does an Amoeba reproduce?
a) Through self-fertilization
b) Through binary fission
c) Through sexual intercourse

18) Are there more male or female Earthworms?
a) More male
b) More female
c) Neither. The earthworm is a hermaphrodite

1. b	2. a	3. a	4. c	5. c	6. b
7. b	8. a	9. a	10. a	11. b	12. a
13. a	14. a	15. a	16. b	17. b	18. c

16

FISH

1) What is the peculiarity of the Cave Fish *(Noemacheilus smithi)* ?
a) It has no external organs
b) It is deaf
c) It is blind

2) Which fish has four hearts, one nostril, no jaws, no stomach and scavenges on dead animals?
a) Hagfish (Myxinidae)
b) Stingray (Dasyatidae)
c) Gulpeᵣ Eel (Eupharyngidae)

3) How many volts of electricity can the Electric Eel *(Electrophorus electricus)* of South America stun you with?
a) 50 volts
b) 100 volts
c) 500 volts

4) What is the Herring family (Clupeiformes) character-ized by?
a) Silvery scales that come off easily

b) Long sharp needle-like teeth
c) Paddle-shaped snouts

5) Bony-tongued fishes (Osteoglossiformes) and marine Catfishes have a characteristic breeding procedure in common. What is it?
a) The females anchor the eggs to a patch of spongy tentacles grown on the stomach during the breeding season
b) They incubate the eggs in the mouth or throat till the youngsters hatch
c) They hang their eggs in little sacs that are attached to the tails of the male fish

6) Why are the Toadfishes (Thalassophryne) so called?
a) They emit a froglike grunt when caught
b) They have wart-like growths all over their bodies
c) They have long thin retractable tongues which they use to catch their prey

7) The Bitterling (Rhodeus) fish lays eggs in an extremely unusual place. Where?
a) Inside the mantle of freshwater mussels
b) Inside the pouch of the seahorse
c) In a cavity round its neck

8) Which is the largest marine Flatfish?
a) The Halibut (Pleuronectidae)
b) The Scaldfish (Bothidae)
c) The Box fish (Ostraciontidae)

9) What is special about a Lamprey?
a) It is the vampire of the fish world, living off the blood of host fish

b) It is the only fish which changes colour when attacked
c) It is the only fish with a completely luminescent body

10) Which fishes can taste with their whole body?
a) Catfish (Siluriformes)
b) Salmon (Salmoniformes)
c) Codfishes (Gadiformes)

11) Which fish has no scales, is born from eggs carried in a kangaroo pouch by the father, changes colour for camouflage and is named after a land animal?
a) The Sea Horse (Hippocampus)
b) The Two-striped Killy *(Aphyosemion bivittatum)*
c) The Mandarin fish *(Synchiropus splendidus)*

12) Which Indian fish attacks wooden boats with its snout?
a) The Arrowtooth Halibut *(Atheresthes evermanni)*
b) The Striped Marlin *(Tetrapturus brevirostris)*
c) The Sand Tiger Shark *(Odomtaspis taurus)*

13) Which are the only fishes to make a nest?
a) Sticklebacks (Gasterosteiformes)
b) Deepsea Squirrelfishes (Ostichthys)
c) Dories (Zeiformes)

14) Why is the Angler Fish so called?
a) It stays motionless for hours seeming dead until a prey comes near and is snapped up
b) It has a luminous lure at the end of a pole suspended over its mouth to catch its prey
c) It keeps its mouth wide open and its small red tongue upright and waving. Prey often mistake it for a worm and enter the mouth

15) Why is the flatfish Left Eye Flounder so called?
a) Because it has only one eye
b) Because both eyes are situated on the left side of the head
c) Because it can only see with one eye

16) Which fish, on being threatened, feigns death by swallowing air and water and inflating its body like a balloon?
a) The Boar fish (Caproidae)
b) The Puffer fish (Tetraodontidae)
c) The True Goby (Gobiinae)

17) The word Pisces refers to only one class of fish. Which is it?
a) Bony fish (Osteichthyes)
b) Sharks, Rays and Chimaeras (Chondrichthyes)
c) Hagfish and Pteraspids (Pteraspidomorpha)
d) Lampreys and Cephalaspids (Cephalaspidomorphi)

18) Why is the Elephant Fish of Tropical Africa so called?
a) It has a long trunk-like snout
b) It is larger than all other fishes in that part of the world
c) It is grey in colour

19) Cod, Mackerel, Plaice, and Pilchards lay eggs that float. How does that happen?
a) The eggs are lighter than water
b) The eggs contain drops of oil that make them buoyant
c) The eggs are tightly bound together in raft shapes

20) What is a Mermaid's Purse?
a) Horny egg cases laid by sharklike fishes attached to seaweed

b) A fish of the Cichlid family
c) The egg-carrying pouch of the Clown Loaches *(Botia macracantha)*

21) In some fish the dorsal fin has been modified. What purposes do the modified fin serve?
a) To transfer venom through its spine
b) It acts as a bait to attract prey
c) It serves as an organ for greater locomotion

22) What kind of fish is the Starfish?
a) It is not a fish but a spiny-skin (Echinodermata) marine animal
b) It is an electric ray (Torpedinoidei)
c) It belongs to the Uranoscopidae family of Stargazer fish

23) Which one of the Flatfish family can produce a chess-board pattern on its body when alarmed?
a) Plaice
b) Lefteye Flounders
c) Scaldfish

24) Why is the Doctor Fish, found on the West Coast of India, so called?
a) It cleans the mouths of other fish of parasites and infected tissue
b) When eaten it aids the digestion of larger fish
c) It has a marking round its neck shaped like a stethescope

25) Most freshwater fishes in India belong to one family. What is it?
a) Carp (Cyprinidae)

b) Dogfishes (Scyliorhinidae)
c) Soles (Soleidae)

26) A popular food fish found in both southern and north-east India remains out of water for a long time travelling on grassy land over long distances. Which is it?
a) Climbing Perch (*Ananbas testudineus*)
b) Sea Horse (*Hippocampus kuda*)
c) Butterfly Gurnard (*Paratrigla vanessa*)

27) Which fish likes lotus leaves, skinned bananas, boiled rice, tomatoes and weeds? In fact it is considered a biological control for garbage-filled and weed-infested ponds.
a) Silver Salmon (*Oncorhynchus kisutch*)
b) Giant Gourami (*Osphronemus goramy*)
c) Milkfish (*Chanos chanos*)

28) Which is the only Indian anadromous fish?
a) Bonito (*Sarda orientalis*)
b) Oil Sardine (*Sardinella longiceps*)
c) Hilsa (*Hilsa hilsa*)

29) Which small freshwater fish are found in the rice fields of western India during the monsoon?
a) The Blue Ling (*Molva elongata*)
b) The Small Mouth Grunt (*Haemulon chrysargyreum*)
c) The Loach (*Lepidocephalichthys hermalis*)

30) What is an anadromous fish?
a) A fish that migrates from the sea to go up river for breeding
b) A fish that changes colour when threatened
c) A species of fish in which the male hatches the eggs

31) Which of these fish are biological controls for mosquito larvae?
a) Minnows
b) Killifishes
c) Sturgeons
d) Herrings

32) Which fish was introduced into India recently from South America only for its larvicidal propensity?
a) The Lizard fish *(Synodus variegatus)*
b) The Black Swallower *(Chiasmodon niger)*
c) The Mosquito fish *(Gambusia affinis holbrooki)*

33) Which true fish found on the eastern and western coast of India have functionless gills, walk on the sand with their pectoral fins and rest on the stems and branches of mangrove plants?
a) Soles (Soleidae)
b) Mudskippers (Gobiidae)
c) Gunnels (Pholididae)
d) Flying Gunards (Dactylopteridae)

34) What is a small-sized carp called?
a) A minnow
b) A capulet
c) A capsule

35) Why are Indian freshwater perches Chanda Nama and Chanda Ranga called glass fish or X-ray fish?
a) Their body tissues are transparent and their bones are visible
b) The powdered extract of their bodies is an essential ingredient in the manufacture of islinglass
c) Their glossy scales look rainbow coloured in the sunlight

36) What is the difference between a poisonous fish and a venomous one?
a) The body of a poisonous fish contains poisons which are harmful when ingested. The venomous fish injects poison into its victim
b) A poisonous fish only injects poison when attacked. A venomous fish actively pursues its victim
c) A poisonous fish's poison is less harmful than that of a venomous fish

37) Which is the most widely eaten fish in India?
a) Pomfret
b) Beckti
c) Trout
d) Salmon

38) Why is the Sucker Fish or Remora so called?
a) It is a parasite of the Sea Anemone
b) It attaches itself to large marine creatures and eats from the bits of fish that escape from their mouths
c) It pulls in its prey through a suction-like mouth

39) How are Suckerfish used to catch turtles in India?
a) They are killed, injected with a mild poison and set out as bait for turtles
b) They are tied to a line, released into the sea and, when they attach themselves to a turtle, both are pulled in
c) Since the sounds they make are identical to the mating calls of the turtle, they are kept alive and pressed for the noise. When the turtle responds it is caught

1.	c	2.	a	3.	c	4.	a	5.	b	6.	a
7.	a	8.	a	9.	a	10.	a	11.	a	12.	b
13.	a	14.	b	15.	b	16.	b	17.	a	18.	a
19.	b	20.	a	21.	bc	22.	a	23.	a	24.	a
25.	a	26.	a	27.	b	28.	c	29.	c	30.	a
31.	ab	32.	c	33.	b	34.	a	35.	a	36.	a
37.	a	38.	b	39.	b							

17
CREATURES OF THE SEA

1) A marine creature has both ova and sperm, produces its own eggs and fertilizes them -- the two stages being known as white sick and black sick. Which creature is this?
a) The Oyster
b) The Electric Eel
c) The Pipefish

2) How many arms does the Giant Squid have?
a) 8
b) 10
c) 12

3) The Walrus *(Odobenus rosmarus)* has two long tusks growing from its upper jaw. What does it use them for?
a) For digging out crustaceans from the sea bottom
b) For defence
c) For scratching away parasites from its body

4) Where are a Whale's nostrils situated?
a) Just above the mouth
b) On top of its head
c) Just above its ribcage

5) How many teeth does a Blue Whale *(Balaenoptera musculus)* have?
a) 842
b) 60
c) None

6) How do Mussels (Mytilus) feed?
a) By coming out of their shells and snatching prey as it passes
b) By drawing in a current of water from which they sieve off the fine organisms
c) By attaching themselves to sea anemones and scraping the arms of the latter for attached organisms

7) The shells of which mollusks were used as warhorns?
a) Triton's Trumpet *(Charonia tritonis)*
b) Bull-Mouth Helmet *(Cypraecassis rufa)*
c) Horn-Coloured Ram's Horn *(Planorbarbius corneus)*

8) The Crab has all-round vision. How does it manage that?
a) It has eyes all over the carapace of its shell
b) Its eyes are on swivelling stalks
c) It can turn its head 360 degrees

9) What is the average weight of a Blue Whale?
a) 30,000 kg
b) 120,000 kg
c) 70,000 kg

10) What is the main food of the Baleen Whale in the Antarctic Ocean?
a) The Blue Crab *(Callinectes sapidus)*
b) The Norwegian Lobster *(Nerphrops norvegicus)*
c) The Oceanic Prawn *(Euphausia superba)*

11) Why does a Whale suffocate when it is stranded on the shore?
a) Due to a weak ribcage its lungs are compressed by its weight
b) It cannot breathe outside water
c) Tiny sand particles are inhaled and enter its mouth and lungs

12) What is the difference between a Shrimp and a Prawn?
a) The true prawn has pincers on its second pair of five legs
b) A small shrimp is called a prawn
c) A prawn shell is spiral-shaped while a shrimp's is crab-shaped
d) There is no difference

13) How many eggs does an average Oyster lay in one year?
a) 1,000,000
b) 500,000,000
c) 230,000

14) Which animal is known as the Minstrel of the Ocean?
a) The Humpback Whale *(Megaptera novaeangliae)*
b) The Great Siren *(Siren lacertina)*
c) The Australian Lungfish *(Neoceratodus forsters)*

15) Which creatures are the direct or indirect food of all the creatures on the ocean's surface?
a) Blennies

b) Plankton
c) Bread Sponges

16) How many calories does an average Blue Whale con-
    sume daily?
a) 80,000
b) 3,000,000
c) 200,000

17) Which of these can whistle?
a) Hawaiian Spinner Dolphins *(Stenella longirostris)*
b) Pilot Whales *(Globicephala melaena)*
c) Narwhals *(Monodon monoceros)*

18) Which marine creature has the ability for rapid mim-
    icry – even of humans?
a) The Walrus
b) The Sea Lion
c) The Dolphin

19) How many 'arms' does the Octopus *(Octopus vulgaris)*
    have?
a) Six
b) Four
c) Eight

20) There have been cases of Octopuses committing sui-
    cide. How do they do this?
a) They beach themselves
b) They devour each arm till they die
c) They block themselves into cavities in the ocean and
    starve to death

21) What is an Oyster larva called?
a) Fingerling

b) Spat

c) Oysterette

22) How does an Octopus camouflage itself?
a) By changing colours to merge with the background
b) By hiding behind rocks
c) By burrowing into the ground

23) What is the Mollusc shell chiefly composed of?
a) Calcium carbonate
b) Chalk lime
c) Silica

24) When attacked, what does a Cephalopod do as a defence measure?
a) It uses its arms to stir up the ocean floor to create a screen
b) It discharges a cloud of ink to distract the attacker while it flees
c) It runs backwards at a very high speed

25) What do the ridges on the shell of the Mollusc signify?
a) They are lines of growth/age
b) Nothing. They are merely a decorative pattern
c) They are warning patterns

26) The ridges on the shell are often uneven in their spacing. What does a wide ridge on the shell of the mollusc mean?
a) Food has been plentiful so the mollusc has added more to the shell
b) The shell has been damaged at some stage and then repaired
c) The mollusc has spent a greater amount of time during that period in the shell

27) What mineral is nacre or mother-of-pearl made of?
a) Salt compressed to form a permanent structure
b) Calcium carbonate
c) Nitre

28) Why is the Sea Cow (Sirenia) so called?
a) It feeds on seaweed and marine grasses
b) Its mating call sounds like the call of a cow
c) Its body is large and fat with six nipples showing
    prominently

29) Which animal is known in India as the *Pani Kutta* or
    Water Dog?
a) The Gangetic Dolphin *(Platanista gangetica)*
b) The Smooth-coated Indian Otter *(Lutra perspicillata)*
c) The Corrugated Frog *(Rana corrugata)*

30) Which animal is used by the Muhanas of Sind as a decoy
    to capture dolphins?
a) The Smooth Indian Otter *(Lutra perspicillata)*
b) The Malabar Flying Frog *(Rhacophorus malabaricus)*
c) The Climbing Perch *(Ananbas testudineus)*

31) What does the male Elephant Seal *(Mirounga leonina)*
    do when it becomes angry?
a) It inflates its nose till it becomes like a large balloon
b) It roars loudly and stands on its tail flipper
c) It inflates its chest

32) Does the shell of the Snail grow with its body?
a) Yes
b) No
c) It depends on the species of snail

33) Which is the largest pinniped?
a) The Crab-eater Seal *(Lobodon carcinophagus)*
b) The Elephant Seal *(Mirounga leonina)*
c) The Southern Sea Lion *(Otaria byronia)*

34) What are the differences between a Seal (Phocidae) and a Sea Lion (Otariidae)?
a) The neck of the sea lion is longer and more clearly marked
b) The sea lion has external ear flaps while the seal does not
c) Sea lions can pull their hindlimbs forwards and backwards to propel themselves on land. Seals cannot
d) Sea lions have furry undersides while seals are completely hairless

35) Snail shells are divided into dextral and sinistral shells with dextral being much larger in number. What is the classification?
a) Shells with ridges are dextral; those without are sinistral
b) Shells that are right-handed in their spirals are dextral, those that are left-handed are sinistral
c) Shells that are inhabited by seashore molluscs are dextral, those that are inhabited by sea-going molluscs are sinistral

36) What is unusual about a Hermit Crab *(Coenobita hilgendorphi)*?
a) The Hermit Crab and the Sea Anemone are the only examples of symbiosis in the sea
b) The Hermit Crab is the only member of its family to live on sea grasses

c) The Hermit Crab does not have its own shell but moves about in the empty shells of whelks that it occupies temporarily

37) How does a Squid move?
a) By pumping water violently out of its body through the siphon it moves by jet propulsion
b) Its ten external limbs act as legs
c) Only the first four of its limbs act as legs, the others push by waving themselves in the water creating a current

ANSWERS

1. a	2. b	3. b	4. b	5. c	6. b
7. a	8. b	9. b	10. c	11. a	12. a
13. b	14. a	15. b	16. b	17. a	18. c
19. c	20. b	21. b	22. a	23. a	24. b
25. a	26. a	27. b	28. a	29. b	30. c
31. a	32. a	33. b	34. abc	35. b	36. c
37. a					

18

AMPHIBIANS

1) The Midwife toad *(Alytes obstetricians)* has an exceedingly curious way of keeping its eggs. What is it?
a) The male makes foam nests on top of leaves where the eggs are laid
b) The female carries the eggs in her mouth till they are ready to hatch

c) The male wraps strings of them around its hind legs and carries them around till they are ready to hatch

2) The Axolotl (Ambystoma) is not an amphibian but the tadpole of the Tiger Salamander. However, some of the tadpoles do not turn into adults, merely growing into large tadpoles and even breeding as tadpoles. Why does it not turn into a salamander in some parts of the world?
a) Wherever the waters lack iodine the tadpole cannot complete its development
b) It needs a temperature of more than 35 degrees Centigrade to complete its development
c) While the tadpole breeds in salt water it needs fresh water to complete its development. Where it cannot make the journey inland to a freshwater lake it remains a tadpole

3) How does a Frog breathe under water?
a) Through its nostrils
b) Through its skin
c) Through its gills

4) What is the difference between a Toad and a Frog?
a) Toads have a dry warty skin while frogs have a fairly smooth, moist skin
b) Toads are exclusively land animals while frogs spend a large part of their lives in water
c) Toads are much larger than frogs

5) The frog is essentially an animal of the water. Where does the Trilling Frog (Neobatrachus centralis) live?
a) By the ocean
b) In the desert
c) By large lakes

6) What scientific oddity does the Pseudis Paradox Frog owe its name to?
a) The tadpole is three times larger than the frog
b) The frog is the only hermaphrodite of the amphibian kingdom
c) The frog is the only non-moulting member of the amphibian kingdom

7) The brood care behaviour of the South American frog *(Rhinoderma darwini)* is singular among frogs. What is it?
a) Both the male and female join in making a nest in the hollow of a tree and the male stands guard till the young are ready to go into the water on his back
b) All the frogs of the species lay their eggs in a common pool and females take turns to guard them
c) When the embryos show within the egg-sacs the male snaps them up into his vocal sac till they come out fully developed from his mouth

ANSWERS

1. c   2. a   3. b   4. a   5. b   6. a
7. c

19

MURDER AND MAYHEM

1) Which deer race, once prolific, has now only a 100 living members left on the shores of the Logtak lake in Manipur?
a) The Brown-antlered Deer *(Eldi eldi)*
b) The Maral *(Cervus elaphus maral)*
c) The Dybowski's deer *(Cervus nippon dybowskii)*

2) Which bird, held sacred by the Egyptians, is now extinct there?
a) The Sacred Ibis *(Threskiornis aethiopica)*
b) The Sacred Kingfisher *(Halcyon sancta)*
c) The Egyptian Reed-warbler *(Acrocephalus stentoreus)*

3) Who wrote this description of the extermination of a harmless Sirenian animal for sport and fur?
a) "They harpooned one of the docile grazing giants and pulled on the hooked harpoon until the animal was exhausted due to massive loss of blood. Those in the boat wore it out with continual blows until, tired and completely motionless, it was attacked with bayonets, knives and other weapons and pulled up on land. Immense slices were cut from the still living animal but all it did was shake its tail furiously. It took thirty men to pull it ashore. If the animal's mate and young followed they were also slaughtered in this way."
a) Ivan Popov
b) Georg William Steller
c) Adolf Eric Norderskiold

4) Which of these birds are now extinct in India?
a) The Little Stint *(Calidris minuta)*
b) The Mountain Quail *(Ophrysia superciliosa)*
c) Jerdon's Courser *(Cursorius bitorquatus)*
d) The Greywinged Blackbird *(Turdus Boulboul)*
e) The Pinkheaded Duck *(Rhodonessa caryophyllacea)*
f) The Ashy Swallow-Shrike *(Artamus fuscus)*

5) The Fennec *(Fennecus zerda)* is one of the most charming looking mammals in the world. Small, shy, with a soft whimpering call and completely harmless to humans as it lives on a desert diet of lizards, locusts,

plants and rodents. It is being hunted to extinction by the people of the Sahara. What is it?

a) A panda
b) A rabbit
c) A fox

6) Which animal, now extinct, was the ancestor of the domesticated donkey?

a) The Nubian Wild Ass *(Aquus africanus africanus)*
b) The Quagga *(Equus quagga quagga)*
c) The Somali Wild Ass *(Equus africanus somalicus)*

7) The Quagga of South Africa is now extinct. What animal was it?

a) A zebra striped on the head, neck, and shoulders
b) A larger relative of the ostrich
c) A member of the Dwarf Antelope family

8) Which animal evolved in North America, moved to Eurasia, becoming extinct in its place of origin where it has to be reintroduced?

a) Horse
b) Buffalo
c) Bison

9) Which species of harmless marine mammal was exterminated by indiscriminate hunting only twenty-seven years after it was discovered?

a) The False Killer Whale *(Pseudorca crassidens)*
b) The Rough Toothed Dolphin *(Steno bredanensis)*
c) The Steller's Sea Cow *(Rhytina stelleri)*

10) Which animal was hunted to extinction in India as recently as 1947?

a) The Snow Leopard *(Uncia uncia)*

b) The Cheetah *(Acinonyx jubatus)*
c) The Black Himalayan Bear *(Selenarctos thibetanus)*

11) Approximately how many species of the animal world will have been wiped off the earth by A.D. 2000?
a) Ten thousand
b) One million
c) One hundred thousand

12) Which of these animals/birds are extinct?
a) The Passenger Pigeon *(Ectopistes migratorius)*
b) The Great Auk *(Plautus impennis)*
c) The Duckbilled Platypus *(Ornithorhynchus anatinus)*
d) The White-footed Tamarin *(Oedipomidas leucopus)*

13) Which animal, believed to have been extinct, was discovered existing along a narrow foothill belt in Assam?
a) The Assamese Flying Lemur *(Cynocephalus alii)*
b) The Burmese Falcon *(Falco rangoonius)*
c) The Pigmy Hog *(Sus salvanius)*

14) There are eight subfamilies of Tiger. Of these how many are now extinct or almost extinct?
a) 7
b) 5
c) 3

15) Which of these Horses are in danger of extinction?
a) Barb
b) Brumby
c) Asiatic Wild Horse
d) Percheron
e) Bullrock

16) Which horse is extinct?
a)   The Darley Arabian
b)   The Clydesdale
c)   The Tarpan *(Equus przewalskii gmelini)*

ANSWERS

1. a	2. a	3. b	4. abe	5. c	6. a
7. a	8. a	9. b	10. b	11. ab	12. c
13. c	14. c	15. ac	16. c		

20
THE LADDER OF CREATION

1)   In which geographical period did birds evolve?
a)   Permian
b)   Silurian
c)   Quaternary
d)   Jurassic

2)   In which geographical period did mammals evolve?
a)   Cambrian
b)   Silurian
c)   Tertiary
d)   Triassic

3)   Which were the dominant mammals of the Mesozoic era?
a)   Pinnipedia
b)   Marsupialia
c)   Proboscidea

4) In which period did fish first appear?
a) Silurian
b) Devonian
c) Permian

5) Which was the dominant species of life during the Mesozoic era?
a) Mammals
b) Birds
c) Reptiles

6) In which era did mammals become important?
a) Cenozoic era
b) Palaeozoic era
c) Mesozoic era

7) What are the dominant species of the Palaeozoic era?
a) Birds
b) Amphibians and insects
c) Reptiles

ANSWERS

1. d   2. d   3. b   4. a   5. c   6. a
7. b

21

WHO SAID IT ?

1) Who wrote the poem which starts:
   'The Owl and the Pussy Cat went to sea
   In a beautiful pea-green boat,
   They took some honey, and plenty of money,
   Wrapped up in a five-pound note.'

a) Edward Lear
b) R.L. Stevenson
c) A.A. Milne

2) What did the third Little Pig build his house of?
a) Sand
b) Bricks
c) Straw

3) Which animal disguised itself as Red Riding Hood's grandmother unsuccessfully?
a) Wolf
b) Fox
c) Tiger

4) Of which animal is this said 'a creature full of opposing qualities, in which the most vigorous energy and composed languor, gentleness and daring, shyness and persistence are all united in one animal'?
a) Gorilla
b) Tiger
c) Panther

5) Who killed Cock Robin?
a) The Sparrow
b) The Hen
c) The Pig

6) Which fish did the poet Oliver Herford refer to when he described it as 'unmixable as vitriol and water – a thing of furs and fins'?
a) Porcupine fish (Diodontideae)
b) Catfish (Siluriformes)
c) Sucking Barbs (Garra)

7) Which bird was Longfellow referring to in 'Evangeline' when he wrote 'from his little throat such floods of delirious music that the whole air and the woods and the waves seem silent to listen'?
a) The Mockingbird *(Mimus polyglottos)*
b) The Abbotts Jungle Babbler *(Trichastoma abbotti)*
c) The Brown Thrasher *(Toxostoma rufum)*

8) In which book are the animals Gryphon, Mock Turtle, March Hare, and Cheshire Cat mentioned?
a) Alice's Adventures in Wonderland
b) Watership Down
c) Grimm's Fairy Tales

9) Who wrote:
'I never nursed a dear gazelle
To glad me with its soft black eye
But when it came to know me well
And love me it was bound to die.'?
a) T. Moore -- 'Lalla Rookh'
b) Idris Shah -- 'The Way of the Sufi'
c) Kahlil Gibran -- 'The Prophet'

10) In which of Shakespeare's plays is the line 'A horse! a horse! my kingdom for a horse'?
a) Much Ado about Nothing
b) King Lear
c) King Richard the Third

11) In which play of Shakespeare are the lines
'Wilt thou be gone? It is not yet near day;
It was the nightingale, and not the lark,
That pierc'd the fearful hollow of thine ear.'?
a) A Midsummer Night's Dream

b) Romeo and Juliet
c) Hamlet

12) What emotion does William Blake refer to in 'The Tiger':
Tiger! Tiger! burning bright
In the forests of the night,
What immortal hand or eye
Could frame thy fearful symmetry?
a) Hope
b) Fear
c) Love

13) In which book are the insects Snapdragonfly, Rocking-horsefly and Breadandbutterfly mentioned?
a) *Systematic and Experimental Zoology*
b) *Through the Looking Glass*
c) *The Lion, The Witch and the Wardrobe*

14) What does the proverb 'Cats hide their claws' mean?
a) The necessity to probe deeper into a problem
b) The need for caution
c) Everything is not always as it seems

15) What does this proverb refer to: 'The higher the ape goes the more he shows his tail'?
a) Pride
b) Stupidity
c) Ill-breeding

16) What does this proverb mean: 'If the lion's skin cannot, the fox's shall'?
a) All means should be adopted to attain a goal

b) Cunning surpasses strength
c) Never give one's true self away

17) What does this proverb correspond to: 'He that makes himself a sheep shall be eaten by the wolf'?
a) All lay load on the willing horse
b) Bear and forbear
c) He conquers who endures

18) What does the Turkish proverb 'Call the bear uncle till you are safe across the bridge' correspond to?
a) Claw me and I'll claw thee
b) Dogs wag their tails not so much in love to you as to your bread
c) As a wolf is like a dog so is a flatterer like a friend

19) What does the proverb 'He that cannot beat the ass, beats the saddle' mean?
a) One who shifts the blame for one's own mistake
b) One who gets one's work done by any means
c) One who tramples over anything to attain one's goal

20) What does the idiom 'Beard the lion in his den' mean?
a) To show unnecessary courage
b) To tackle a problem foolishly
c) To face an adversary on his home ground

21) What does the idiom 'Flogging a dead horse' mean?
a) To show unnecessary cruelty
b) To try to achieve something impossible
c) To bring up forgotten matters

22) What is 'a big frog in a small pond'?
a) An important person among small people

b)   One who talks a lot
c)   One who can be heard amongst a crowd of people

23) What kind of person does the phrase 'bull in a china shop' describe?
a)   a clumsy person
b)   an out of place person
c)   an ill-mannered person

24) Which animal has given rise to the idiom 'Bury one's head in the sand'?
a)   The Sandpiper bird
b)   The Sand Rat
c)   The Ostrich

25) What do you do when you cook someone's goose?
a)   Feed them well
b)   Ruin them
c)   Steal from them

26) What happens when you go to the dogs?
a)   You deteriorate
b)   You get bitten
c)   You fall ill

27) Of which creature did Plutarch write 'It is the only creature that loves man for his own sake'?
a)   Monkey
b)   Dog
c)   Dolphin

28) Who was the author of this verse on the food chain:
'So, naturalists observe, a flea
Has smaller fleas that on him prey;

174

And these have smaller fleas to bite 'em,
And so on ad infinitum'?
a) Jonathan Swift
b) Rupert Brooke
c) Edgar Allan Poe

29) Who was Senator Joseph McCarthy referring to when he said, 'It looks like a duck, walks like a duck and quacks like a duck'?
a) John F. Kennedy
b) A communist
c) A duck

30) Which fictional character said 'I am a Bear of Very Little Brain and long words Bother me'?
a) Yogi Bear
b) Winnie the Pooh
c) Smokey the Bear

31) Which book has the sentence 'All animals are equal but some are more equal than others'?
a) *Animal Farm* by George Orwell
b) *My Family and Other Animals* by Gerald Durrell
c) *In the Belly of the Beast* by Jack Henry Abbott

32) Who was the author of the fable 'The Hare and the Tortoise'?
a) Enid Blyton
b) Aesop
c) Shakespeare

33) Which famous zoologist and anthropologist said 'The city is not a concrete jungle, it is a human zoo'?
a) Gerald Durrell

b) Desmond Morris
c) Virginia Woolf

34) About whom did Winston Churchill say 'A sheep in sheep's clothing'?
a) Clement Atlee
b) Ramsay MacDonald
c) Edwina Mountbatten

35) Who said 'Horse sense is the good judgement which keeps horses from betting on people'?
a) Karl Heinrich Marx
b) W.C. Fields
c) Charles Chaplin

36) Which famous poet is the author of the verse:
   'God in his wisdom
   Made the Fly
   And then forgot
   To tell us why.'?
a) W.B. Yeats
b) Robert Frost
c) Ogden Nash

37) In which poem did the killing of an Albatross lead to death and disaster for the ship's crew?
a) 'Morituri Salutamus' by Longfellow
b) 'The Rime of the Ancient Mariner' by Coleridge
c) 'Rover's Song' by Eliza Cook

ANSWERS

1. a	2. b	3. a	4. b	5. a	6. b
7. a	8. a	9. a	10. c	11. b	12. a
13. b	14. b	15. c	16. b	17. a	18. a

22
FACTS AND FANTASY

1) Which bird was considered in European mythology to deliver human babies?
a) The Peruvian Booby *(Sula variegata)*
b) The Eurasian White Stork *(Ciconia ciconia)*
c) The Christmas Frigate Bird *(Fregata andrewski)*

2) Which world conqueror's horse was named Bucephalus?
a) Julius Caesar
b) Alexander
c) Napoleon

3) What did the gorgon Medusa have growing on her head instead of hair?
a) Snakes
b) Lice
c) Worms

4) In the Bible, which creature swallowed Jonah?
a) The Giant Squid
b) The Whale
c) The Lion

5) Which animal is on the crest of the kings of England, Scotland, Norway and Denmark?
a) Unicorn
b) Lion
c) Leopard

6) Which animal was used by Hannibal to cross the Alps in 218 B.C.?
a) The Tarpan Horse
b) The Elephant
c) The Camel

7) Where and when was the first zoo created and what was it called?
a) China. 12th century A.D. Garden of Intelligence
b) Galapagos Islands. 11th century A.D. World of Wisdom
c) France. 8th century A.D. The Royal Enclosure of Animals

8) Which insect was part of the religious mythology of Egypt attaining great significance as a talisman?
a) The Scarab Beetle *(Scarabaeus sacer)*
b) The Small Emperor Moth *(Saturnia pavonia)*
c) The Hornet Moth *(Aegeria apiformis)*

9) The Golden Fleece that Jason brought back from Kolchis to Greece was probably the fur of which animal?
a) The Sable *(Martes zibelline)*
b) The Woolly Hare *(Lepus oiostolus)*
c) The Golden Jackal *(Canis aureus)*

10) Which animal known for its playfulness and affectionate temperament was used by Indian princes for hunting?

a) The Brown Bear *(Ursus arctos)*
b) The Indian Brown Mongoose *(Herpestes fuscus)*
c) The Cheetah *(Acinonyx jubatus)*

11) Which Emperor of India issued edicts protecting animals and forests and making game and fishery laws?
a) Ashok
b) Aurangzeb
c) Itmad-ud-daulah

12) Which animals did the Pied Piper of Hamelin drive away?
a) Cockroaches
b) Swallows
c) Rats

13) Which animal formed the head of the sceptre of the Pharaohs in early Egypt?
a) Dog
b) Cat
c) Lion

14) Which animal was made a Roman Senator by Caligula Caesar and actually took his place in the Senate?
a) Dog
b) Monkey
c) Horse

15) *The Mahabharata* mentions an animal as a teacher of Yudhisthira. Which one was it?
a) The snake
b) The mongoose
c) The elephant

16) Which animal accompanied Yudhisthira and his brothers on their last journey?
a) Dog
b) Eagle
c) Deer

17) A team of which animals pulls Santa Claus's sled?
a) Mountain Pyrenees dogs
b) Reindeer
c) White horses

18) What is the Zodiac sign of Taurus represented by?
a) Ox
b) Bull
c) Elephant

19) Which animal was declared by the Prophet Mohammad to be his favourite animal?
a) Cat
b) Horse
c) Camel

20) Who is the mythological Hindu Lord of Bears whose daughter married Krishna?
a) Rukmin
b) Jambavan
c) Bhaleshvara

21) Who is considered the Hindu mythological Lord of the Birds?
a) Garuda
b) Jatayu
c) Aruna

22) Which creature was responsible for having Adam and Eve thrown out of Eden?
a) Snake
b) Monkey
c) Crocodile

23) Which animal is considered an embodiment of cosmic power in the Vedas and the four elephants that support the earth rest on it?
a) Tortoise
b) Eagle
c) Lion

24) Which creature represents the Zodiac sign of Pisces?
a) Whale
b) Fish
c) Unicorn

25) How many stars are there in the constellation known as the Great Bear?
a) 7
b) 6
c) 5

26) What is the Zodiac sign of Cancer?
a) Crab
b) Spider
c) Chameleon

27) Hanuman is the Hindu monkey god. What does the word Hanuman or Hanumat mean?
a) Long-tailed
b) The strong-jawed
c) Hairy man

28) What is the steed of the Hindu God of Love Kama?
a) Pigeon
b) Parrot
c) Deer

29) Who is the Bengali goddess of snakes?
a) Vaijayanti
b) Jagadambika
c) Manasa

30) What is the steed of Yama?
a) Buffalo
b) Tiger
c) Vulture

31) What animals are considered the chariot pullers of Ushas, the Hindu Goddess of the Dawn?
a) Grey doves
b) White swans
c) Red cows

32) Which obstacle-removing god of Hindu mythology is elephant headed and what is his mount?
a) Ganesha -- Rat
b) Garuda -- Eagle
c) Garga -- Pig

33) Which is the steed of Brahma?
a) The Hansa Swan
b) The Mithun Bull
c) The Zebu Cow

34) Which is the steed of the planet Mercury personified as Budha?
a) Lion

b) Porcupine
c) Bear

35) What is the emblem of the founder of Jainism, Mahavira?
a) Lion
b) Horse
c) Peacock

36) Which animal's head does Anubis, the Egyptian god of the afterlife, have?
a) Eagle
b) Jackal
c) Snake

37) In Hindu mythology which animal is the steed of Indra?
a) Horse
b) Elephant
c) Eagle

38) What is the Zodiac sign of Leo represented by?
a) Cat
b) Tiger
c) Lion

39) Whose mount is the Peacock?
a) Kartikeya
b) Saraswati
c) Dharma
d) Brahma

40) Which creature forms the couch of Vishnu?
a) The Snake

b) The Iguana
c) The Tortoise

41) Which is the mount of the Telugu Goddess Ammavaru?
a) Cow
b) Jackal
c) Lion

42) Which is the creature representative of Aphrodite, the Greek goddess?
a) Dove
b) Unicorn
c) Dolphin

43) Which animal is supposed to have suckled Romulus and Remus, the founders of Rome?
a) The lamb
b) The wolf
c) The goat

44) What is the Centaur of Greek mythology?
a) Half man-half deer
b) Half man-half horse
c) Half man-half goat

45) Which is the steed of the Bengali goddess of smallpox, Shitala?
a) Pig
b) Ass
c) Tiger

46) Which animal carried Mary to Jerusalem?
a) Donkey
b) Horse
c) Cow

47) Where was Jesus supposed to have been born?
a) In a stable
b) In a pigeon coop
c) Neither

48) Which is the steed of Shiva?
a) Ram
b) Ox
c) Bull

49) Which animal is sacrificed by Muslims on the day of Id?
a) Goat
b) Dog
c) Camel

50) Which Egyptian statue has a lion's body and a human head?
a) Sphinx
b) Tutankhamen
c) Aspis

51) Which animal represents the Zodiac sign of Aries?
a) Pig
b) Ram
c) Dog

52) Which creature represents the Zodiac sign of Scorpio?
a) Snake
b) Scorpion fish
c) Scorpion

53) Odin is the old German God of War, patron of heroes and lord of the Valkyries. Which are the animal and bird sacred to him?
a) Wolf, Raven

b) Lion, Eagle
c) Tiger, Owl

54) What was the name of Rana Pratap's horse?
a) Lakshmi
b) Chetak
c) Rajput

55) Which mythical bird is considered the sympol of eternal life for its ability to resurrect itself from its own ashes?
a) The Golden Goose
b) The Phoenix
c) The Kestrel

ANSWERS

1. b	2. b	3. a	4. b	5. b	6. b
7. a	8. a	9. d	10. c	11. a	12. b
13. a	14. c	15. b	16. a	17. b	18. b
19. a	20. b	21. a	22. a	23. a	24. b
25. a	26. a	27. b	28. b	29. c	30. a
31. c	32. a	33. a	34. a	35. a	36. b
37. b	38. c	39. a	40. a	41. b	42. a
43. b	44. b	45. b	46. a	47. a	48. c
49. a	50. a	51. b	52. c	53. a	54. b
55. b					

23
ODDBODS

1) Our clothes affect our mosquito appeal. The lighter the colour of our clothes, the less mosquito bites we are likely to have. Is this statement true or false?
a) True
b) False

2) Which ugly, large-nosed creature is known locally by the name meaning White Man?
a) The Proboscis Monkey *(Nasalis larvatus)*
b) The Proboscis Bat *(Rhynchonycteris naso)*
c) The Lowland Tapir (Proboscidea)

3) Sea Cows or Dugongs were mistaken right up to the twentieth century for mermaids. Why?
a) Their call sounds exactly like the shrill scream of a woman in distress
b) Female sea cows rise vertically out of the water holding their young in their arms and feeding them from the two prominent nipples on their breasts
c) Before they became wary of hunters they often swam on their backs close to boats and only their mammae could be seen

4) Which animals keep a babysitter for their young who manages the kindergarten and prechews their food?
a) Apes
b) Elephants
c) Hyena

5) An old and popular, though fallacious, belief is that domestic dogs will become wilder if crossed with wolves.

The Institute for Domestic Animals in Kiel has conducted studies hybridizing wolves with dogs, the end result being known as a Puwa. Which dog has been used?

a) The Siberian Husky
b) The Poodle
c) The Weimaraner

6) What are Dead Man's Fingers *(Alcyonium digitatum)*?
a) Branches of polyp coral structures
b) Arctic plankton
c) The stringy excreta of the dolphin family

7) Tigers and crows are the most abundant of the creatures of this order in India. What species are we referring to?
a) Butterflies
b) Carnivorous Bats
c) Stick insects

8) Which creature's songs are the longest and the most intricate known to man -- in fact they have even been marketed as records?
a) The Broadbilled Hummingbird *(Cyanthus latirostris)*
b) The Humpbacked Whale *(Megaptera novaeangliae)*
c) The Golden Oriole *(Oriolus oriolus)*

9) Which animal spends most of its life hanging upside down from trees?
a) The Flower-faced Bat *(Anthops ornatus)*
b) The Entellus Langur *(Presbytis entellus)*
c) The Common Two-toed Sloth *(Choloepus didactylus)*

10) Which animal's voice is said to be a combination of the bark of a small dog and the hoot of an owl?

a) The Jackdaw *(Corvus monedula)*
b) The Pallas' Cat *(Felis manul)*
c) The Orangutan *(Pongo pygmaeus)*

11) Which animal's urge for freedom is so great that if trapped and confined to a narrow cage it will literally die of fright?
a) The Ermine *(Mustela erminea)*
b) The Antelope Jack Rabbit *(Lepus alleni)*
c) The Kite Fox *(Vulpes macrotis)*

12) Which animal has such a mania for salt that it will even eat sticks of dynamite?
a) The Canadian Porcupine *(Erethizon dorsatum)*
b) The White Spoonbill *(Platalea leucorodia)*
c) The Sand Wallaby *(Wallabia agilis)*

13) Which of these creatures detaches its tail as a method of escaping from its predators?
a) The Tokay *(Gecko gecko)*
b) The Jollytail fish *(Galaxias maculatus)*
c) The Tuatara *(Sphenodon punctatus)*

14) Which creatures capture slaves and make them work at collecting food and grooming the nest while they lounge around doing nothing?
a) Jet Ants *(Lasius fuliginosus)*
b) Amazon Ants *(Polyergus rufescens)*
c) Red Ants *(Formica rufa)*

15) Which member of the animal world chooses his mate by dropping a pebble at her feet – and sometimes, because it is difficult to make out the sex – at an insulted male's feet?
a) The male Penguin (Spheniscidae)

b) The male Lesser Panda (Ailuridae)
c) The male Sand Grouse (Pteroclidae)

16) One marsupial's fur has such colour variability that in one season alone, one million of these creatures were killed in Australia and their fur exported as chinchilla, skunk and beaver. Which animal is it?
a) The Koala Bear
b) The Brush Tailed Possum
c) The Hare Wallaby

17) Which creature can look in two directions simultaneously?
a) The Alligator (Alligatoridae)
b) The Agamid (Agamidae)
c) The Chameleon (Chamaeleontidae)

18) Which animals are considered engineers and builders, famous for their elaborate airconditioned houses made of logs, stones and mud?
a) Beavers
b) Moles
c) Weaverbirds

19) For many years dentures were made of a certain animal's teeth, more in demand than the elephant's tusks because they did not turn yellow. Which animal was this?
a) The Blue Whale
b) The Hippopotamus
c) The Camel

20) During World War II the Americans planned to send this creature as living incendiary bombs into enemy

territory. The plan did not work because of the raven-
ous appetite of the creature. What is it?
a) Pigeon
b) Dolphin
c) Bat

21) Of which animal can it be said that its philosophy is
simple -- if the creature facing you is smaller, eat it. If
bigger, run from it. If it is the same size, mate with it?
a) The Chihuahua
b) The Frog
c) The Praying Mantis

22) Which type of cloth are mosquitoes least attracted by?
a) Thick silk
b) Luminescent satin
c) Pure linen

23) Which animal changes its coat colour and name in
winter?
a) Stoat, brown – to Ermine, white
b) Kangaroo rat, brown – to Mink, white
c) Squirrel, red – to Sable, white

ANSWERS

1. a	2. a	3. b	4. b	5. b	6. a
7. a	8. b	9. c	10. b	11. d	12. a
13. a	14. b	15. a	16. b	17. c	18. a
19. b	20. c	21. b	22. b	23. a	

24
NOT TIRED YET?

1) The turtle can deliver a nasty bite. How many teeth does it have?
a) 14
b) 8
c) None

2) Reptiles have one major feature that birds and mammals don't. What is it?
a) They continue to grow till they die
b) They moult their skins frequently
c) They have retractable nails on their limbs

3) Which of these has a brain that is 31% smaller than the other?
a) Dog
b) Wolf

4) Which of these is not a Bear (Ursidae)?
a) Koala Bear
b) Brown Bear
c) Polar Bear

5) Which of these can attain the maximum height of 100 cm?
a) Wild Boar
b) Dog
c) Lion
d) Tapir
e) Tiger

f) All of them
g) None of them

6) What is the difference between a Bull and a Bullock?
a) A bullock has a shorter and thicker neck
b) A bull is black, a bullock is cream coloured
c) A bullock is a castrated bull

7) Which car is nicknamed Beetle or Bug?
a) Volkswagen
b) Citroen
c) Jaguar

8) Which was the first animal to go into space?
a) Dog
b) Cockroach
c) Ape

9) Of all the domestic animals which is the only one that
    does not live in social groups?
a) The horse
b) The cat
c) The dog
d) The turkey

10) What is the order in which the Leopard eats his prey?
a) Liver
b) Kidneys
c) Heart
d) Nose
e) Tongue
f) Eyes

11) A Lion's prey is not always killed by the Lion himself. Sometimes he may take a prey killed by another animal. In what percentage is it?
a) 75% is killed by the lioness, 12% by other cat predators and 12% by himself
b) 40% is killed by the lioness, 50% by himself, and 10% by other cat predators
c) 10% is killed by the lioness, 60% by himself, and 30% by other cat predators

12) What is a pachyderm?
a) A thick-skinned non-ruminant ungulate
b) An animal with four knees and hooves
c) A four-footed carnivore with long hair

13) Which animal has become the symbol of the practice of medicine?
a) Goat
b) Snake
c) Hyrax

14) What is the largest division of the animal kingdom?
a) Arthropoda
b) Chordata

15) What is an arthropod?
a) A creature with an external skeleton and paired jointed legs
b) A creature with an internal skeleton and paired jointed legs
c) A creature which uses limbs for propulsion

16) What is the animal whose skeleton makes coral called?
a) Polyp

b) Coralite
c) Reefer

17) What is a Flying Fox?
a) A fruit bat
b) A flying squirrel
c) An extinct species of fox

18) Which mammal is known in Hindi as the *susu* ?
a) The Gangetic Dolphin *(Platanista gangetica)*
b) The Common Trinket Snake *(Elaphe helena)*
c) The South Indian Rock Lizard *(Psammophilus dorsalis)*

19) Which creature spreads influenza to horses?
a) The Horseflea
b) The Rat
c) The Horsefly

20) Which animal types have the most advanced foot posture for running?
a) Unguligrade animals such as elephants, pigs, cows, and horses
b) Plantigrade animals such as man, monkeys, and bears
c) Digitigrade animals such as dogs and cats

21) In which animal have the toes been reduced to one?
a) Kangaroo
b) Elephant
c) Horse

22) Why does the Sloth look green?
a) It has green fur
b) It has tiny algae coating its fur
c) It has iridescent fur

23) Which animals are described by these colours -- palomino, bay, chestnut, golden dun, paint?
a) Pigs
b) Pheasants
c) Horses

24) Which of these is a living fossil?
a) Fossil Giant Duck *(Cnemiornis)*
b) Coelacanth *(Latimeria chalumnae)*
c) Sea Mouse *(Aphrodite aculeata)*

25) Which animal is normally given a wide berth by lions and bears because of its sharp defence armour?
a) The Porcupine
b) The Tasmanian Devil
c) The Hedgehog

26) Which animal defends itself by squirting a noxious liquid called mercaptan which suffocates and temporarily blinds its attacker?
a) The Shrew (Soricidae)
b) The Skunk (Mustelidae)
c) The Civet (Viverridae)

27) Which animal, regarded as one of the most intelligent of the animal kingdom, washes its food before eating it?
a) The Chimpanzee (Pongidae)
b) The Raccoon (Procyonidae)
c) The Domestic Cat (Felidae)

28) Which is the only non-mammal to have a diaphragm?
a) Crocodile
b) Tuatara
c) Monitor Lizard

29) Which animal's local Hindi name is *kasturi* ?
a)   The Small Indian Civet
b)   The Musk Deer
c)   The Himalayan Weasel

30) Large flaps of skin joining the front and hind limbs
    allow this animal to glide and parachute from tree to
    tree. Which animal is this?
a)   Flying Squirrels (Pteromyinae)
b)   False Vampire Bats (Megadermatidae)
c)   Hutias (Capromyidae)

31) Which is the main sense used by insects and animals in
    courtship?
a)   Sight
b)   Touch
c)   Smell

32) Which animals use an ultrasonic sonar to detect their
    prey?
a)   Pit vipers
b)   Bats
c)   Screech owls

33) What do the Owl and the Sloth have in common?
a)   They both sleep more than 16 hours of the day
b)   They are the only two animals who can turn their
     heads 180 degrees
c)   They are the only three-toed animals

34) Which is the only animal with four knees?
a)   The Elephant
b)   The Alpine Ibex
c)   The Okapi

35) What are Trogons?
a) Birds of tropical forests
b) Non-flying birds of the ostrich family
c) Dinosaur ancestors of the lizard

36) What is the best-known example of symbiosis in the
    animal world?
a) The Hermit Crab *(Coenobita hilgendorphi)* and the Sea
    Anemone *(Calliactis parasitica)* which attaches itself
    to its shell
b) The Mediterranean *Carapus acus* which lives inside
    Sea Cucumbers
c) The worm *Ascaris lumbricoides* which lives inside the
    domestic pig

37) What is the main way to get rid of a pest infestation of
    the home?
a) Pesticide
b) Cleanliness
c) Dust filters

38) What is the best way to tell the difference between a
    butterfly and a moth?
a) Butterflies are colourful, while moths are dull
b) Butterflies are diurnal, while moths are nocturnal
c) Butterflies have club-shaped antennae while moths
    have plume-shaped antennae

39) Of what species of fish is the Goldfish an ornamental
    variety?
a) Carp
b) Herring
c) Salmon

40) What is the most abundant species of bird in the world?
a) The House Crow
b) The Red-Billed Quelea
c) The House Sparrow

41) What do bats and dolphins have in common?
a) Both navigate through echo-location
b) Both need a constant humidity and temperature
c) Both have one flying variety

42) Where do Penguins live?
a) North Pole
b) South Pole

43) How can you tell the difference between Frogspawn and Toadspawn?
a) Frogspawn is laid on water, toadspawn on the ground
b) Frogspawn is laid in clumps, toadspawn in long strands
c) Frogspawn is white, toadspawn is yellow

44) When was Project Tiger launched in India?
a) 1947
b) 1972
c) 1964

45) What is the difference between a Possum and an Opossum?
a) An opposum is an American marsupial and the possum is an Australian one
b) Opossums are arboreal and possums are not
c) The opossums are polyprotodont whereas the possums are diprotodont

46) What do African Elephants and Baboons have in common?

a) They are the only African animals that dig holes to find water
b) Both have a special fondness for the leaves of the Baobab tree
c) Both have a large red patch under their tails that grows lighter as the animal matures

47) What do the Elephant, the Hippopotamus and the Rhinoceros have in common?
a) They are all pachyderms
b) They are all in danger of extinction
c) They are the three largest land animals in the world

48) What is a Zebroid?
a) A member of the vulture family which has zebra-like markings on its wings
b) A description of any species of animal that has vertical stripe markings
c) A cross between an ass and a zebra

49) Is the zebra pattern
a) Black stripes on white?
b) White stripes on black?
c) White and black stripes on brown?

50) Which animal comes first in a dictionary?
a) aardvak
b) aakmòa
c) aardvark

51) Which of these is not a mythical animal?
a) The Dodo
b) The Unicorn
c) The Yeti
d) The Loch Ness Monster

52) Why is Donald Duck wrongly named?
a) Because the comic strip actually shows a goose
b) It should be Donald Drake

53) You have heard of a skunk. What is a Skink?
a) A female skunk
b) A small, ground-dwelling lizard
c) A bue skinned rodent

ANSWERS

1. c	2. a	3. a	4. a	5. f
6. c	7. a	8. a	9. b	10. abcdef
11. a	12. a	13. b	14. a	15. a
16. a	17. a	18. a	19. b	20. a
21. c	22. b	23. c	24. b	25. a
26. b	27. b	28. a	29. a	30. a
31. c	32. b	33. b	34. a	35. a
36. a	37. b	38. c	39. a	40. b
41. a	42. b	43. b	44. b	45. a
46. a	47. a	48. a	49. a	50. c
51. a	52. b	53. b